STARLIGHT BASIN

STARLIGHT BASIN

Giff Cheshire

SAGEBRUSH
Large Print Westerns

First published in Great Britain by Chivers Gunsmoke
First published in the United States by Random House

Published in Large Print 2005 by ISIS Publishing Ltd.,
7 Centremead, Osney Mead, Oxford OX2 0ES
United Kingdom
by arrangement with
Golden West Literary Agency

British Library Cataloguing in Publication Data
Cheshire, Giff, 1905–
    Starlight Basin. – Large print ed. –
    (Sagebrush western series)
    1. Western stories
    2. Large type books
    I. Title
    813.5'4 [F]

    501485262

    ISBN 0–7531–7302–6 (hb)

Printed and bound in Great Britain by
T. J. International Ltd., Padstow, Cornwall

TO CRAIG AND CRETE
my motive power

CHAPTER
ONE

Lex Starlight looked into the brightness of the street windows and stopped the old Washington press. A teenage boy had cut past and swung to a panting halt in the doorway. Blood smeared a sweaty cheek, his hair was gray with dust and a broken gallus strap dangled to a bony knee. But Lex saw only the eyes of Jimmy Kemble, puffed, darkening flesh about craters of wrath.

"Who was it?" Lex said, and the sound punched across the room at the boy.

"Hap Haber. I met him coming into town when I crossed the bridge. He took a paper away from me. He read your editorial and went wild."

A girl watched from a back table where she folded papers. She started to move forward, then changed her mind. Lex could only wait as Jimmy came on to him. He saw the boy's lower lip, which looked like a burst cherry. Deep in the sealed places a man calls his soul something stirred and was sick. The outward damage was trivial to Jimmy; his hurt was in that same recess within himself. The world held no more important work to Jimmy Kemble than delivering the *Call* each week.

"I reckon the papers went in the crick," Lex said when Jimmy could get no more out.

Nodding and swallowing hard, Jimmy held forth what he carried. It was a cut-down gunny sack he used to carry the papers. He tried to speak but could only swallow convulsively again. Lex took the sack and looked into it, and the burn in his own eyes went deeper.

"Haber said to give that to you," Jimmy managed to say. "And tell you it's all you print in the *Call*, anyhow. He dumped the papers and scooped up a whole pile of horse manure. I couldn't stop him."

"I know that, Jimmy."

Lex walked to the cold sheet-iron stove and stuffed the sack into it. He pulled a block of sulphur matches from his pocket and set fire to a summer's accumulation of waste paper. He left the stove door open and watched, disregarding the belching flames, as the filthy sack caught fire and was consumed. His hands were trembling, and his broad upper lip was pulled tight across his teeth.

"And another thing, Lex," he heard Jimmy saying. "Haber said they're set to knock your political crusade in the head for good. He sounded mighty confident about it."

"We knew it would be mean, Jimmy. And it'll get worse before election."

"He's over in the Wagonwheel. I watched to see where he went."

Lex did not respond to that. He saw that Sara Jerome was watching him across the last of the week's edition, which she was folding. Her eyes said so clearly: *Your hat's on the nail. Haber's still in town. What's holding you back?* The smelly, overheated printing shop was very quiet.

"You go home," he told Jimmy, "and let Amy fix you up. If she thinks you ought to see Doc Cornell, you go. We'll have more papers ready by the time you get back."

Jimmy looked stunned at the complete passivity of the editor's face. Sara appeared on the point of saying something to him, then she changed her mind. Jimmy held some kind of grudge against her, and she sensed that he did not want her partisanship. The boy turned and went out.

"Poor kid," Sara said then.

"Yeah. He must have given Haber a tussle, at that."

"He'd fight anything on earth in defense of the *Call.*"

Lex put a look of such flat temper on her that she lowered her gaze and fell back to work. She was a dark girl, a little tall, but slender and supple in shape. Her eyes were brown and always more eloquent than her low-pitched voice. Often they invited, again they repelled and all too often they rebuked him as now.

Hap Haber was an outlaw from Slick Ear Plateau, one of many cogwheels in the corrupt political machine ruling the county. Gunhawk and fistic mauler — and Sara and Jimmy were not the only ones wanting something done about the obscene insult to the fighting little *Call.* The machine would like nothing better than for its editor to give Haber a chance to eliminate him from the coming campaign.

But that was not what held Lex back. He was a shock-haired man with the Starlight rawboned height. His was a wire-rope kind of thinness, honed down by a lifetime of hard work. He was not an editor at all but a cowpoke trying to run a newspaper for a sick man — for Big John Starlight, his father. Big John had first come into the country and founded the cattle business in the basin. He was a man respected and loved — and had made his son Lex promise to fight only through the little weekly paper.

Extra papers were ready for delivery by the time Jimmy returned. Lex would have taken out this printing himself except for the look lingering in Jimmy's face. It would add insult to injury to take him off his job because it had grown rough. Lex gave him a slap on the shoulder and told him to get at it.

When Jimmy had vanished around the corner, Lex got his hat. Sara didn't say anything as he headed for the door, but her eyes brightened with curiosity. And he said nothing at all, himself.

Heat vibrated from the dust of the street and danced on the high rim beyond the town. As his boots thumped solidly on the rough plank walk, Lex looked at Flat Rock and liked what he saw. When Big John drove his first stockers onto basin grass, there had been nothing here. For a long while afterward there had been only a crossroad store. Now the town was the county seat.

4

Physically, it seemed a pleasant, honest and open town. Tall shade trees and trim gardens set off the mixture of brick and frame buildings that had sprung up over the years. Shirt-sleeved men and women in house dresses mingled in seeming indolence on the streets — and yet some were rich from the country's honest opportunities as well as from political graft.

Willow and cottonwood fringed the river and the creek that came into it on the edge of the settlement. In the distance rose the foothills of the scattered Rockies, dark and timbered and lifting to white-capped peaks. The cow country stretched out into several broad, flat valleys but was no longer the mainstay of the town. Nesters had come in even greater proportion, and in the years of corrupt government a heavy criminal element had tinged the whole.

Well down the street from Lex, Trink Jenkins came out the door of the Wagonwheel saloon, wiping his mouth on his sleeve. He turned toward Lex in slack-gaited indifference then, noticing him, straightened and hurried forward.

Coming up, he made a nervous grin. He was a scrawny, stubble-faced man and some people said he was better than the town's two newspapers for getting the news around. He ran one of the livery stables.

"Hap Haber," Jenkins said breathlessly. "He's drinking in the Wagonwheel — and talking. He's telling how he sent you enough horse manure to fill up your next issue. But if you're looking for him, Lex, forget it was me who told you. I don't want Haber after me. That jigger is pure poison."

"That isn't where I'm heading, Trink," Lex said.

"It ain't?" The stableman looked astonished. "Lex, he's got the boys laughing their heads off about it."

"Anybody who can laugh at that can hop to it, Trink."

Lex strode on, aware of Jenkins' unbelieving stare on his back, out of eyes like Sara's, like Jimmy's. Anger made its acid crawl through his own flesh. Ask Jenkins to declare himself in public as to how he would vote in another six weeks, and the man would clam up tight.

The same was true of every other businessman down the length of this street. Lex remembered what a time Big John had had in finding men with the courage to form an opposition slate to go up against the long-entrenched machine. Later, with the filing accomplished, there had been the matter of distributing the placards printed on the *Call*'s old job press. Nobody had had window space for them, for fear rode this Wyoming town like an invisible gas.

Such meetings as had been held by the opposition had been brought together in secret, as if a criminal rebellion were being plotted. That in itself was an affront to Lex Starlight, a mockery of men's right to meet, discuss and promote their views. It was a double insult when such men were the pioneers in the county, men who had turned it from wilderness into vigorous, prosperous country. Let Haber call their views — as expressed through the *Call* — anything he wanted, and let the men the paper sought to help laugh about it.

Pacing thoughtfully, Lex put another sudden interest on the street ahead of him. Henny Cobb, of Horseshoe out in the cattle basin, had emerged from the Wagonwheel, his wizened features twisted into a black scowl. Observing Lex, he changed his mind about crossing the street and swung around and waited.

As Lex came up, Cobb jerked a thumb over his shoulder at the saloon and said, "I had to get outta there before I got my head knocked off."

"I know," Lex said. "The hell with Haber."

"Somebody's got to turn his wick down, though," Cobb said darkly. "I've watched elections come and go ever since Staff Palgrave come here and took over the county. Derision's a mighty powerful tool, Lex. Palgrave's always used it against our reform tickets. But not against Big John. Nobody ever laughed at John Starlight and got away with it."

"Damn it, Henny," Lex exploded, "it's not just a matter of going in there and shutting Haber up. That big son never does a thing except in Palgrave's interest. He's trying to turn it into a dirty fight, the kind they can always win."

"But he's hurting us. Lex, you know that."

"I know it," Lex admitted. "Henny, you've been at the meetings John's held in his bedroom. You know what he says."

"Ought to," Cobb said dryly. "John's said the same thing at every election and lost on it every time. That we've got to upset the machine through the kind of decent practice that Palgrave despises. Forget I mentioned it, Lex. I know you're over a barrel."

"A position," Lex said, "that I don't think I'm going to be able to hold much longer. How's things out in the basin?"

"Nothing ever changes out there. But, thank God, it's the kind of place that don't need changing. Tell John hello for me. I'll come up and see him the next time I'm in town. Holly's doing fine running the ranch, but we miss you out there, Lex."

"Sure wish I was back," Lex said. "But John says the only campaigning we can do is through the *Call*. It's not needed out in the basin, which is all we've got behind us. It would be useless on Slick Ear Plateau, where everybody lives off of outlawry, anyhow. As for the nesters — they haven't forgotten the trouble when they first come into the country, and you know what John's doing about them. So I'm stuck here a while, printing John's paper and swallowing things like Haber just pulled."

Cobb held out his hand: "I know how tough it is, Lex. And that it's going to get tougher yet. Let us know any time you need us, for anything at all."

CHAPTER
TWO

Lex Starlight angled across the street and took the corner-cut door of the Flat Rock *Daily News*. A brick structure housed the plant, about which hung an air of dignity and specious propriety. No stranger would even suspect its complete servility to Staff Palgrave, while no local resident would for a moment doubt it. The steam machinery was rumbling and hissing as Lex walked through the door, for the daily issue had gone to press. Lex looked around.

A man at a roll-top desk in the outer office stared at him and drew thoughtfully on a cigar. He seemed discomfited by the heat, belligerent and yet indifferent. Lex tipped him a cool nod that brought no exchange, then went on through another doorway that stood across from him.

There was another man at a desk by the street windows who gave him an irritated, impersonal glance that grew into recognition and an annoyed stare. "Howdy, Frank," Lex drawled. "Seen your bully boy lately?"

Frank Renwick, the *News*'s editor, was getting fleshy, but the solid weight of a healthy, active man still dominated his frame. In addition to running the daily paper, he was one of the county commissioners soon to face the voters again. He was middle-aged; his crinkly hair was turning gray. His eyes, wide and steady, were now lively with truculence. He was a dangerous man, physically and professionally, and Lex had never discounted that fact.

"Your talk," said Renwick, "is about as clear as the way you write. Just who do you mean by my bully boy, may I ask?"

"Who else but Hap Haber? Judge Palgrave's tough hand, just as you're the one in the velvet glove."

Renwick studied that, then snapped, "Get to the point, Starlight, and then get out of here. We run a real newspaper, and I'm busy."

Lex grinned and came on into the room. "I see you've got a copy of today's *Call* there," he said. "I'm flattered, Frank. I didn't know you read my paper."

Renwick frowned at the slim little newspaper on his desk. "One of the boys brought it in to me for a laugh. It sure gave me one, Starlight. New papers and amateur editors always like to start a political crusade — even when they have to invent the issues, like you're trying to do. Sometimes it helps their circulation. Again, it gets them into real trouble. While politics go right on, Starlight, as they always will. Now — why that reference to Hap Haber?"

"All right, we'll play like you don't know. He threw most of my town edition into the river. That's not so bad, but he roughed up Jimmy Kemble. Maybe you don't know that he steamed up enough to sound off. He said something about Palgrave being set to hurt me.

That ties right in with your little threat, just now." The press stopped at that moment so that the silence became sharp, eloquent.

Renwick's surprise seemed genuine — his annoyance was plainly so. "Why come to me with that?" he asked. "Go see Haber — or Palgrave, if you insist on linking them up. Your smelly little rag isn't important enough for me to have a hand in a thing like that. I can answer your editorial charge in kind. I don't have to throw it in the river."

"When Haber spills threats," Lex said promptly, "it means new dirty work's afoot, or he wouldn't know about it. He's not the Judge's brains department — you are. What's up?"

Renwick's continuing uneasiness convinced Lex that Haber had tipped a hand he was not supposed to reveal. The man meditated for a moment, then said, "Haber gets all kinds of wild ideas. You know that, and so does everybody else. I have no idea what he was driving at — if he said what you claim. But you are asking for trouble, man. You're making wild, loose talk in that sheet of yours. That editorial, today, on what you called the Palgrave Principle of Perpetuity could get you sued for all you and Big John have got. The Judge is tolerant, but one of these days he's apt to do it."

"I don't print what I can't prove is true," Lex said. "What I said in that editorial is news to nobody. I only tried to clear up muddled thinking and offset some of the dissembling your paper always does for the Judge. Staff Palgrave once told Big John that he could keep himself in office forever if he pleased fifty-one percent of the voters at the expense of the other forty-nine. With election coming, I figured it was time the voters were reminded of that. It only takes a swing of two percent, you know, and I'm after it."

"Through sheer distortion," Renwick returned. "If Palgrave ever made a remark like that he was talking about something else, and Big John used it for a smear. And if Haber got rough about that smear, I don't blame him."

Somebody spoke from the doorway.

"What are you two quarreling over?"

It was an affable voice, deep and rich, a stentorian tone that had spellbound voters for two decades. Lex turned to see Staff Palgrave come in. The man carried a creased copy of the little *Call* but was actually smiling at Lex.

"So I got another reader I never counted on," Lex said.

Palgrave tipped his head, still smiling. "Let me congratulate you on a sharp editorial, Lex. Only I've got a notion you stole the whole idea from Big John, if he didn't dictate it outright."

"He did."

"What's this about being somebody's tool?" Renwick cut in with a faint sneer.

"At least Big John's name goes on the masthead as publisher."

So long the county judge that even his enemies instinctively associated man and office, Stafford Palgrave was tall, white-haired, pink-jowled. But Lex knew that his portly look was entirely deceptive.

Although tailored and barbered to a flawless finish, Palgrave had fists that could knock down a man his full size and half his age. As a campaign stunt, he liked to flip a silver dollar into the air and smash it with a .45.

As long as he had known the man, Lex still was not sure whether that outer amiability was reflected inwardly. The man was an instinctive politician. On the other hand, he was so well heeled financially and entrenched politically that he did not have to be pleasant unless he chose. Therefore he seemed to be the breed of frontier cat who could be ruthless on the one hand and mawkishly sentimental on the other. This duality fooled a great many people, at least the fifty-one percent of the county's population that Palgrave needed to keep supporting him.

Now Palgrave smiled at Renwick and said, "Why the glower, Frank? There's no real quarrel between you and Lex Starlight. It's always been me and Big John and it still is. But we're both old now and quarreling through you two."

There was enough truth in the remark so that Lex shrugged, but he saw anger leap into Renwick's face. The editor and county commissioner liked being called unimportant even less than he liked the reference to his servility.

"One of these days, Judge," said Renwick, "I might decide to talk for myself."

"Why don't you? I've always wondered what you'd say."

"Now, look here . . ."

Ignoring him, Palgrave swung his attention back to Lex, saying, "I'm glad Big John's got the fight in him for one more campaign. A fine slate he's worked up against us, this time. Doc Cornell for my job — that choice is shrewd. There's hardly a man in the county that doesn't love old Doc for something he's done over the years. I love him myself."

"But you'll destroy him," Lex said, "along with the rest of the slate."

"That's right."

"Well, remember that, this time, there's a newspaper that can talk back."

"Oh, I'm not forgetting the *Call*, misguided though it is. It's a pity Big John doesn't have journalistic talents to equal his political savvy. Take the choice of Tom Lerner for Renwick's job on the commission. Tom's so well honored that he's really got Frank worried. I don't blame him. I've got a notion to vote for Tom, myself. He draws a lot of water on the nester flats, where our main strength lies. He'd do me as well as Frank. The way it lies, Tom and Doc give Big John a pretty strong hand." Palgrave edged his hips onto Renwick's desk, knocking over an inkwell. Since the ink ran away from him, he didn't get up.

"It's a strong hand," Lex said. "And you're making a mistake, Staff, if you plan to start rough stuff — particularly of the variety Hap Haber seemed to be referring to."

"What's Haber been saying?" The Judge kept smiling, but suddenly it was under glacial eyes.

14

"First, do you know that he put the town edition of the *Call* in the river, today?"

Palgrave gave Renwick a long look, then said, "The damned fool. Did you have a hand in that, Frank?"

Renwick's face was still angry. He threw up his hands. "You're Hap's love, Judge. He doesn't come to me for orders."

"I thought you were trying to kick sand in my eyes," Lex said to Palgrave. "Are you fool enough to think you can scare the *Call* out of business?"

Palgrave studied him, and something in his eyes told Lex that he had been considerably annoyed by Haber's threatening outburst. The man shook his head. "You've got a fine little weekly, Lex. It's good for us to have an opposition paper. Keeps us on our toes. In fact, I like your paper well enough that I'd like to talk with you if you ever decide to retire from the business. I might run the *Call* myself just to keep Frank awake."

"I'll bear that in mind," Lex said. "Maybe after the election you'll need the job."

He nodded to the two and walked out, satisfied that Haber had not been talking through his hat. Something was coming, and it would be rough or Hap Haber would not have been in on it . . .

Two horsemen came into town with a clatter. Lex stopped at the edge of the sun-yellowed walk when he recognized his brother Holly with Pitt Berts. The pair spotted him at the same time, squinting at him against the sun. They swung over the dust to the walk along the side of the *Daily News* building. They remained in the saddle.

The three grinned in pleasure for they had all grown up together. Pitt was segundo at Toadstool, the Starlight spread which Holly had run since Big John took to his bed. Now Pitt was the candidate for sheriff on Big John's carefully selected slate, a thing the young puncher had undertaken only for the sick man's sake.

Holly Starlight had Lex's rangy build, but his hair was brick-colored, his movements faster, his eyes more restless. Dust-mixed sweat now stood on his brown face. Palgrave's dig about John Starlight running his sons applied to Holly, too — the wildling whom Big John handled with a Spanish bit. Holly was a drifter at heart, with a strong taste for excitement, but his life had known only hard work. Discipline was the breath of life to Big John, a discipline he applied to himself before he asked it of others. But neither son had been happy in it after coming of age.

"What're you boys doing in town so early in the day?" Lex asked. "Electioneering?"

"Come after shells."

It was Pitt who answered. He was short and chunky, with straw-colored hair and a square jaw. In their boyhood he could lick either of the Starlight boys, but then as now he would die for either more readily.

"Shells?" Lex said sharply, wondering at the bit-off way Pitt spoke.

"Rustlers," Holly said. "The first in a long while. They made a real heavy cut on us, last night. I'd say around forty head. Pitt and me rode sign as far as Pilot Rock. Any fool could figure out where the beeves went from there."

"Where?" Lex asked.

Pitt grinned at him. "Come out and take your own look. It might make a nice story for your newspaper."

"I'll be out," Lex promised.

He was interested. He knew that Pitt was referring to Slick Ear Plateau, which supported a bunch of shoe-string cattle outfits, a bleak and broken stretch of range lost in the foothills. For a generation it had been the hideout of a drifting outlaw element that had been such a plague under Palgrave's crooked administration.

The strip lay above the main basin, on the eastern boundary of the Starlights' Toadstool. The basin had suffered heavily through the years, with little or no help from the sheriff and his force of deputies.

"You going up to see Big John?" Lex said to Holly.

Holly shook his head. "I reckon not, this trip. Big John always manages to guess when something's eating on me, and he can always worm it out. You know what he'd say about us boys going after them rustlers ourselves." Holly dropped his voice to resemble Big John's yeasty roar. "By God, it don't matter a hoot who's running the law in this country! The law's still here! The more we take it into our own hands the more lawless things get! We got to respect it, and we got to elect a sheriff we can respect along with it!" There was bite in Holly's voice. Many of Big John's strictures were poor subjects for jokes.

Pitt made a little bow. "Which breed of hombre now sets before you, gents."

Holly grinned at him. "One thing's sure. If you ever get that star pinned on your shirt, you're going to be a busy man for a while."

"You mean when he gets it pinned on," Lex said. "Holly, you better pay Big John a visit before you go home. He'll hear you've been in town, and the next time he sees you he'll peel you good."

"Besides," said Pitt, "there's Amy."

"When it comes to her," Holly said, "you've got more of a point. Maybe I'll be up later, Lex. If I don't show up, you come out tomorrow." With Pitt following, he angled his horse across the street toward the hardware store, to go after their ammunition.

The sun was throwing long shadows, reminding Lex that it was close to supper time. But it had been a long while since he had felt much appetite and his decision to go home now came from Big John's eagerness to see each new issue of the *Call* as it came out. It had been his idea to start the opposition paper.

Returning to the *Call* office to pick up a copy and wait for Jimmy to come in from his interrupted delivery, Lex found that Sara had finished her work. She looked tired, for this was the heavy day of the week, and she looked depressed. Daughter of the town's new veterinary, she did not seem to belong in Flat Rock. Boredom had caused her to seek employment and, except on press days, her main duty was to tend the office and gather news and advertising. She had been a help because she was well educated and knew how to curry the paper. When Lex entered, she was seated at his desk, idle, and the late light from the window touched her softly.

"Jimmy hasn't come back yet," she said, "but I guess he must have got along all right, this time. Why do they let Haber hang around this town so openly? Everybody knows he's been in the pen and ought to be there yet."

"It wasn't this county that sent him up," Lex said. "He's safer here than he'd be in the owlhoot, even. He's Palgrave's choreboy, and everybody knows it. He gets Palgrave a lot of votes, the ones that have got to be scared into the corral. He's also the go-between for the county officers and the wild bunch on Slick Ear Plateau."

"I was wondering why he's never taken to task."

Lex straightened. "That was aimed at me. You won't rest till I've punished him for the paper business, will you?"

She gave him a level look. "I certainly don't like to see a bully get away with it. Especially when the victim is Jimmy Kemble."

"Fighting Haber is risky."

"Admitting that you're afraid of him?"

Her eyes, flatly on him, were suddenly taunting. An impulse came up in him in a wild surge. He reached, ignoring the sudden alarm in her eyes, and he lifted and brought her across his knee. He delivered a dozen stinging slaps to her posterior while she kicked and struggled in an incongruous silence.

He stood her on her feet finally and said, "Don't play with a man's feelings. You've got no idea what you're fooling with."

Her face was stretched in disbelief. Her eyes smoldered. She rubbed the back of her dress and gasped.

"Well," she breathed, finally. "How do you like that?"

"Fine," he said. "How did you?"

"So you found a way to let off steam without the risk of taking up for Jimmy with Hap Haber."

"I'll do that when it suits me — not you."

"All right," she said, relenting a little. "I suppose I shouldn't have crowded you. But I loathe Hap Haber. He comes to my house right along."

"Been bothering you?"

"He would, except for Dad. And someday he's going to catch me alone. That's why it annoys me to see him get away with anything he wants."

"That sounds like more sic 'em."

"Oh, I don't expect you to worry about me."

She had him beat. She liked to arouse him, first one way and then another. Sometimes he thought that to be only the normal interest of a young woman unattached. She had been much pursued ever since coming to Flat Rock, not too long ago, yet had taken up with none of the available men. But she was a woman of full feeling, for hints of that were always close to the surface of her face.

Still stinging, he said, "Well, you can't blame Haber for that interest, anyhow. You make any man who looks at you paw the ground."

"Well — thank you."

"I don't mean that you try," he said quickly.

"Never mind," she said, with a trace of bitterness. "I guess we've both had mistaken ideas."

"Sara . . ."

He reached out and placed his hands on her arms, surprised at the extent to which he had offended her. Confusion wormed in him, for he knew all at once how right she was about his mistake. What he had taken for a natural flippancy, even flirtatiousness, had been something else, something deeper, and he had shamed her by revealing the true nature of his interest in her.

She pulled back, but suddenly he realized it was not because of him. He turned to look at the doorway and let his arms go slack. Jimmy stood there. His face was stony as he came on in and hung his sack on a nail. All three were caught in a silence in which Lex could hear the water from the faucet drip into the sink.

"Hungry, kid?" Lex said feebly. "Let's go home to supper."

Jimmy shrugged. He did not look at Sara, whose cheeks were flaming now. Suddenly Lex wondered if he knew why there had always been that coolness on Jimmy's part toward her. Amy, his sister, was Big John's nurse and housekeeper. And Jimmy was old for his years. He must have noticed Lex Starlight's straying eye here in the office. Yet Jimmy was not old enough to realize that a man could want one woman for a while, another forever. He probably could not feel the fiery things in Sara that called to a man so strongly.

"Come on," Lex said roughly. "Let's go eat."

CHAPTER
THREE

Jimmy's battered face drew attention on the way home, and Lex realized that word of Haber's vaunted triumph over the little *Call* had spread all over town. Flat Rock was waiting and wondering, as Sara and Jimmy had waited, to see what Lex Starlight would do. The stress began to push at Lex again. He thought, *Tonight I'll have it out with Big John. He's got to let me out of the promise I made not to start a free-for-all. When he sees Jimmy's face it might change his mind about how to deal with the political machine . . .* The futility of that hope ran through him. Like things had happened before, and Big John had never changed his attitude, his stubborn contention that to maintain clean law in the county its leading figures had first to obey it themselves.

Amy Kemble was setting the table for supper, and the dining room light was softened by vines at the window so that her slim figure was indistinct. She smiled a guarded greeting as he came in from the hallway. There was something in her expression that caused him to hand the paper to Jimmy and watch him bound up the stairs to Big John's bedroom.

Then Lex went on into the dining room, knowing that she had been deeply upset by Jimmy's trouble with Haber. He said, "Don't let it worry you, Amy. Haber won't try that again."

"You know Jimmy's too young to be drawn into a fight with Palgrave, Lex."

"Would you like to send him out to the ranch for a while?" Lex asked. "Jimmy would like it. He gets along fine with the boys out there. And it worries me the way he'll risk his neck sometimes — like he did trying to fight Haber. I think we ought to get him out of the way, some way that won't hurt his feelings, till after the election."

Amy shook her head. "He's always been with me. He'll stay where I am. But I was surprised that you let him carry that paper, knowing it might bring trouble from several different men."

"Now look. I'm not going to whet Jimmy's appetite by telling him something's too dangerous for him. You know that kid as well as I do."

"Just the same, he's only a boy."

Amy's motherlike concern for her brother had always seemed strange to Lex. Small and with plainly dressed yellow hair, she was the older by only a few years. She had reason to worry, however, for their father had been killed by Slick Ear rustlers only a year back. She knew what could come from them, from Haber and the machine here in town.

Then the wonder came to Lex if Amy might not be moving to the ranch soon, herself. She and Holly hit it off, and his visits to the Starlight town house were to see her as much as his father. She had never warmed to Lex, seeming to want to hold him off, although she must have known for a long while that she was the woman he wanted once he was free to take a wife.

Staring at her, Lex reflected that while the appeal of Sara was mainly animal, that of Amy came in good part from the spirit. She was fine-textured, and her brown eyes were warm. Her body was slim and ripe with promise. Yet he could not imagine himself seizing her with the hunger he had felt for Sara not an hour past.

She flushed under his steady study and looked away. Her aloofness had as much told him that if it was to be either of the Starlight sons, it would be Holly. Even Big John thought that it had ought to be Holly. "She's just what he needs," he had once reflected. "She handles him as easy as Jimmy, and she's about the only one who can handle either of them."

Now Lex said, "Well, I don't think he'll get into any more trouble," and knew that it sounded forced and false.

"Sometimes I think that's all life is, Lex." Amy went out to the kitchen, from which came the smells of supper. She had provided the only real home life that Lex could recall, and he watched her wistfully.

He washed up, for he wanted his father's undivided attention when he went upstairs. He waited until Jimmy came running down, hunger having finally drawn him back. The boy's eyes avoided Lex. He was still angered by what he had seen at the printing shop and his interpretation of it. He certainly did not seem to share Lex's opinion of how the wind blew with his sister.

Lex ascended the stairs and entered Big John's room. His father had opened the new *Call* and, holding it to the window light, was now reading it. He nodded absently to Lex and kept on reading until he had finished the editorial that had aroused so many people. He made a big bulge in the bed and, canted against the propped pillows, his upper body still showed its old power. His face was Holly's, with the lines deepened and the eyes faded. But he had Lex's shock of hair.

John Starlight grinned when he put down the newspaper. "We did a good job on that piece, didn't we?" he asked.

"The credit's all yours, John," Lex said. "I wrote it the way you said to." He thought of Staff Palgrave, hearing the man saying to Renwick: *Big John runs Lex and I run you* . . . Irritation bit at Lex as he frowned at his father. He took the straight-back chair at the head of the bed.

Big John said, "What's this about Haber abusing Jimmy?"

"It looks like Jimmy told you."

"He told me. What have you done about it?"

"Nothing."

"Good — and don't. We've got Palgrave on the jump, and there's nothing he'd like better than to bait us into a knock-down-and-drag-out scrap that would cloud the real issues. Haber don't count. You forget him."

"Jimmy counts."

"I know," Big John said patiently. "I explained it to Jimmy. This fight's got to be on the real issues and not some sudden outburst over an incident — dirty as it was."

"John, you've got a hell of a lot more moral courage than I have."

Slowly the big, bedridden man shook his head. "I dunno about that. I feel like you do, too. With no election coming up, and could I get out of these blankets, I might tend to Hap Haber, myself." He sighed.

Lex found himself relenting. Big John was no more an easy mark than he was a physical coward, and many a man had learned that. If anybody knew the fearless, iron will in him, his own sons did. When a heart attack had felled him, six months ago, Doc Cornell had ordered a long rest period. And Doc had known just how to handle John. "You'll never take it," he had said. "You don't have the kind of stuff. You'll cheat on me within three weeks and in three months you'll be dead and buried." Big John had sworn at the doctor, but this was his seventh month of total inactivity up here. He had never once tried to cheat.

"Just the same," Lex said, "I want you to let me out of the promise I made when I came to town to run the paper for you. You know I didn't really want to, any more than Pitt wanted to run for sheriff or Doc for county judge. We did it to please you, to help in something that's been your big ambition since I was a tadpole. But you're making it too tough for us. Moderation's fine, and I know in my heart that you're right about that. But there's a place where a man can't take any more without hitting back."

26

"You're hitting back. Harder than you seem to figure, or they wouldn't be trying to turn it into their kind of a fight. All you want right now is revenge. That never bought a man a thing. It's cost plenty of people hell. Forget it."

"I want a free hand," Lex answered. "And I wish you'd rely more on my judgment. I'm not a fool, and I don't think I'd let Palgrave work me into any whipsaw that would be to his advantage. Just the same, I think today's business calls for more than a debate in the papers. I want to show this county our party won't take the kind of stuff Haber pulled."

John Starlight's eyes grew vacant. "We could have gunned this county clean a long while ago, son — when Staff Palgrave first took over. But it's no good. I said then we had to beat him fair and square or it won't stick, and I still say it. Palgrave knows that. It goes a long way back, Lex — farther than you can remember."

The man's voice had grown almost wistful. There was no self-pity in him, and he rarely referred to his physical condition. But Lex knew that his mind had gone back to his younger, active days, back to things that were a mystery because they had happened before his sons were born. More than once Lex had suspected that there was something there — in that period — that Big John had never divulged, something that still bore upon the stubborn, one-sided fight with Staff Palgrave.

But Lex could remember one thing out of that time about which Big John had talked a good deal. Maybe it was part of what he was trying to avoid by keeping this campaign fight on the highest possible level. Once tempers were aroused and guns started crackling, a range could become a bloody bog overnight.

Below Starlight Basin and its cattle operations ran the wheeling sweep of Kinsey Flats, along the river, entirely taken up now by farmers. At the start, when the railroad first began to promote the settler movement in the country, there had been no such segregation. All the range was open to homesteading, and the nesters had picked the best, indifferent to the fact that it had long been used for cattle range.

The nester movement had been so heavy, so relentless, that it had brought on the inevitable war. The dispute had been settled only by the help of the cavalry, summoned to back the law and therein the nesters. Staff Palgrave had been in that war, his gun hired to the Johnny-come-latelies, and he had come into political power in the backwash of the struggle.

He still sided with the nester element, and conditions had steadily worsened for the cattlemen. The settling movement had cost the grazers their outrange and foisted a constant irritant upon them. But, in an endeavor to offset that, the nesters had been induced to segregate themselves and colonize on the flats. Both sides had been left dissatisfied, so that the old quarrel always simmered.

Big John had fought and bled and lost in that war, and the basin that bore his name still held many like him. None of them had forgotten, for they had never been allowed to forget. It was from the nester colony and the crooked stockmen in the hills that Palgrave drew most of his support. He had never hesitated to sacrifice the cattle country to those special interests.

John Starlight certainly seemed to be thinking of this, his eyes unconsciously revealing an old truculence. Then suddenly he took a long look at his son.

He said, "I'll hold no man to a promise he's come to regret. I knew this was shaping up, and maybe I was wrong trying to tie your hands like I did. You can't profit by another man's experience. Nobody can. But if you don't mind, I'd still like to run this political campaign. And I'd like you to bear something private in mind. Let hellfire break out in this country, and Holly'll be in the thick of it. You know him."

"You trust him even less than me, don't you?"

"That's a fact. He's stubborn, notional and more restless than a man ought to be. Give him a chance and he'll get into real trouble. I never spoke of this before, but I've got to now. Your mother had a brother Holly's the spit and image of. Looks like him, even, with the red hair and smoky eyes. And your uncle — George Galtry — he wound up bad. I've always been scared for Holly."

"Never even knew I had an uncle," Lex said, astonished.

"He was about Holly's age when he went wrong. Last I knew of him he was on the dodge for a stage stick-up he had a hand in. No need of it, either. He was working, drawing down good wages. Just wanted the excitement of it — the way Holly craves it."

Lex looked at his father and said, "I've got something to say to that, John. Holly don't know what you've been scared of. You could drive him over the edge just trying to save him from that. Bedamned if I'd want to force any man to behave himself. That's Holly's decision — one he's got a right to make for himself. The same as I want to make mine as to how I'll meet my problems."

"You're a free man," John said, and he sounded tired. "Take it onto your own shoulders, then. I'd rather consent in advance than have you turn against me, son."

"I wouldn't do that, John. But I guess I was trying to warn you."

Amy, at that moment, came in with John's supper tray. Lex went out, leaving them to badger each other the way they liked to, John pretending to have no appetite until Amy had bullied him to a point where he could give way to a strictly uninvalid-like appetite. That was one of the many things Lex liked about Amy Kemble. Big John had got the blistering of his life the first time he had tried to bring her to heel.

When he got downstairs, Lex found that Holly had come in quietly and was in the big kitchen. Although he usually showed Amy his gay side, he now looked moody and in-turned.

"Get your shells?" Lex asked. He studied his brother, noting the characteristics Big John said had also been George Galtry's: the red hair, the smoky eyes, the eternal restlessness.

Holly groaned. "Easy there. Big John can hear a bird belch a mile away. But Pitt went on home with the what-it-takes. You be out in the morning if you want in on it."

"I want in and I'll be there."

Amy came down smiling to herself, which meant she had scored another victory over John Starlight. John's words ran through Lex's mind, his opinion that she was the only one who could handle Jimmy and Holly. *And maybe you too, John — and me.* In the space of a year she had become the woman's influence in all their lives, a needful role in every family and one that she fit perfectly.

She had been shaped to the part. Even before nature had wrought the changes in her body, she had had to become a woman. Her mother died in the year of the big epidemic that hit central Wyoming. And her father, who had run one of the little satellite outfits on the borders of the big Toadstool, had been killed by rustlers, somebody he jumped in the night. It was not surprising that Amy had a timeless quality within herself, a private source of wisdom and strength. Age of that nature had little to do with the fall of the years.

"Supper's ready," Amy said. "Let's eat."

Holly gave her a slow grin. "You make a lot of extra work for yourself, eating in that dining room when you've got a kitchen table so handy to the stove and sink."

"I never had a dining room before," Amy said. "I mean to make the most of this one."

"There's one as big out at Toadstool," Holly said. "We got a lot of horse gear stored in it. But I'll clean it up when you move out there."

A flush grew in Amy's cheeks. "I've seen it. You use it for poker games, too. There must be a thousand cigarette burns on that beautiful old table of your mother's."

"It can be fixed. Just you say the word."

"I've got no say about Toadstool," Amy said. "If you want to cut up a beef on that table, it's none of my business."

"Wrong there." Holly was enjoying the color in her cheeks. That was Holly, and Lex doubted that he had ever spoken to her seriously of marriage. The man was either afraid of his feelings or afraid of declaring them to a woman until he was sure of where he stood.

Lex felt the bite of a sudden irritation. To needle Holly, he said, "Amy's dug in where she is and likes it. And if she wants that table at the ranch, we'll haul it to town. So don't you go digging out the old house just yet."

Holly shot him a quick, nettled frown. Then he tried to grin but didn't quite make it. There was no doubt that jealousy had stirred him, too, and this was the first evidence of such a feeling in either of them.

"Let's have supper," Amy said in haste.

CHAPTER
FOUR

Lex left the house immediately after supper. His talk with Big John had loosened some chronic tension within himself so that he went forth feeling the rise of an as yet indistinct impetus. He was thinking of George Galtry and the wild streak that had been in the family so long, with neither himself nor Holly aware of it. What Big John did not seem to know — at least had not intimated — was that his older son was not devoid of that wildness, himself.

Flat Rock was serene at this time of early dusk, the supper hour which had closed the business houses and emptied the streets. Now only a few cow ponies were strung along the slick-worn hitch bars. The wagon of some late-traveling nester from the flats was drawn up before the Wagonwheel saloon while its driver fortified himself for a long ride home. The late stage had deposited a few passengers who, with other wayfarers, now occupied the porches of the hotels. The shadow of the high cliff was a creeping blackness across the town. Somewhere beyond the river a dog barked steadily.

Lex found that Sara had locked the *Call* office and gone home. He paused at the door, key in hand, and abruptly decided against entering. A buckskin horse, moving at a slow and nervous trot, had crossed the intersection at the end of the block. Lex saw that it carried Hap Haber. When in town the man kept his horse at Jenkins' livery, which was on up that side street. Shoving the key ring back into his pocket, he swung on down the walk.

He thought, *John's right. Haber's only a tool. Bait in a bigger play by bigger men. If you're smart you won't strike at it* . . . And he remembered other words, coming from Big John, *Let hellfire break out in this country, and Holly'll be in the thick of it* . . . Yet without pause he turned the corner, smooth-walking and steady.

Hap Haber still sat his saddle at the livery door where he talked with Jenkins. Something caused him to look toward Lex, and his big body stiffened. Haber's swart, heavy face wore a look of caution and truculence, the latter heightened by an old scar that gave one eye a squint. But he sat as motionless as the horn on his saddle. The three men were the only ones on this side street, which was graying in the crawling dust.

Lex came up to the mounted man and stopped. He said, "Haber, step down from that horse," and in the moment felt all his restraint let go.

Haber looked along the street, one eye squinted almost shut, then readily threw his weight onto a stirrup and came down, heavy and deliberate. The conversation broke off, Jenkins stirring uneasily in the barn door's obscure light. Haber was armed. From

34

where the liveryman stood it was impossible to tell if Lex was.

Haber dropped the reins, looked at Lex long and hard, then hitched his belt. "Now what, Starlight?" he asked, and something rose in his eyes, an ugly and heated impetuosity.

Lex hit him so suddenly that the man went back against the stallion. It was a punch brought in high, driving to a thudding impact on the underslope of Haber's jaw. It was almost enough. The stallion swung away, the hostler catching the reins and leading it out of the way. Haber nearly fell, then got his feet planted, his legs braced and his thoughts straightened out. He started back.

He took a striding, hunched lunge at Lex. One after another his fists thumped in. Standing firm, Lex caught a blow on his elbow and shunted it off. He smashed Haber full in the belly and felt his fist meet solid flesh. Haber grunted and pain flickered briefly in his face. Anger crowded up through his habitual sneer. Again he pushed in, using short and vicious blows. Grappling suddenly, he tried to smash a knee into Lex's crotch.

Lex got hold of him, pinning both the man's arms beneath his own. He wrenched Haber off his feet and they crashed. Haber hit on his head and shoulders, Lex swinging on top and driving his fists against the man's sweaty head. Haber's fingers clawed into the straw-littered dust. He got to his knees under Lex's full weight. Ramming back with an elbow, he caught Lex hard in the shortribs, knocking the wind out of him.

35

Haber rolled, propped himself and kicked out violently. Lex took a thudding boot in his belly and felt a retching spasm drive through him. He caught the foot but Haber jerked it free. Then the man was scrambling up. Before Lex could rise, Haber sprang in a broad jump, his heels coming down on Lex's chest. The residual air left Lex's lungs in the crush, making him gasp noisily for breath. When Haber began a pile-driving stomp, Lex realized it was meant to maim, to kill.

Catching the man's legs, he let Haber's own weight throw him down. Again Haber hit hard. Lex was astride him, pouring in punches that would have knocked a frailer man apart. Haber heaved, somersaulted and was back on his feet. Lex shoved to a panting stand, tired, knowing that he could not absorb much more of the man's drive. The swirling dust blinded and choked him. He was aware that he had to finish the fight soon or be finished in it. They stared at each other, both knowing that. Jenkins, watching, knew it, too, and slowly rubbed his long jaw.

Haber charged Lex, head lowered, arms driving in steady blows brought up from his hips. Each jolting thud drove Lex farther back. He could not stop Haber; he could only draw off. Then the barn wall put an end to retreat. Haber tried to nail him against it, increasing the tempo of his raining punches. Using the wall for a catapult, Lex sprang back. Haber had expected him to drop in his tracks. He was wide open for a split second. Lex used that fraction of time. He felt a crushing jolt in his knuckles, its jar rolling up his arm. Haber didn't even put out his hands to break the fall. He landed hard. He was not clear out, but he did not try to get up.

Lex hit him in a flat, scaling dive. He heard air gust out of Haber's mouth. The man wrenched. Getting on his chest, Lex used his knees to pin the fellow's shoulders to the littered dirt.

"Man's hungry," he panted to Jenkins. "Fetch me a biscuit."

"Not me!" Jenkins bleated. "I don't want any part of this!"

Lex saw what he wanted in the dust. He reached and got it. He used the flat of his hand to smash it against Haber's mouth.

"Compliments of Jimmy Kemble," he gasped and climbed to his feet.

He walked away and presently was moving along the empty main street, trying to dust himself off. Reaching the entrance of the *Call*, he went in and locked the door behind him. It was dark inside the building, and he lighted one of the office lamps, then carried it to the back of the room so he could wash and inspect the damage.

A look at the mirror showed a puffed eye that would soon discolor, a cut lip that had already grown out of shape. Yet he felt little beyond the soreness the mauling had put in his flesh. That was physical, and his mind and emotions seemed reluctant to grasp what had happened. It gave him a sense of detachment, a kind of cool inner vision. He remembered again, but only briefly, that Big John wanted to win the fight at the polls, that maybe it was John's last chance to do it. Lex brushed that aside. What had happened between him and Haber had been personal. It could not spread if he used caution, and maybe there was a way to see to that.

When he stepped into the street again, he crossed at the corner and went along the thoroughfare that ran over the bridge. Beyond the stream, he swung right toward the section where the town's more pretentious houses huddled together in detached snobbery. They were Flat Rock's best and occupied by the shady and influential in the county seat. It was a section that Lex rarely visited, but he knew where he was heading now.

Judge Palgrave's big residence occupied a spacious area that lay on the edge of the river, a place no county judge could afford to build and maintain. It was kept guarded at all times. Lex was stopped at the gate but got through readily by saying, "The Judge expects me." The sentry's acceptance of that indicated that Palgrave was home.

Then, to a hard-faced man who met him at the door of the house, Lex said, "Ask Palgrave if he still wants to buy a newspaper." The man looked suspicious, then disappeared. He was back at once. He jerked a thumb and stood aside for Lex, still scowling.

Lex crossed a wide hall over a carpet that sank under his boots and went on through an archway where he saw Staff Palgrave in the room beyond. His back to a cold fireplace, the politician had his hands behind him. He was chewing thoughtfully on a cigar as he watched Lex come forward, a battered, rumpled and angry-looking visitor.

Palgrave took the weed from his lips, saying, "Good evening, Lex. You show Big John's cunning. You don't mean to sell your paper — you only asked if I still want it. Transparent to a veteran, of course, but good enough to get you in. What can I do for you?"

"I came to make an appeal, Palgrave — and maybe a bargain."

"So?" Palgrave said and was really interested.

Bluntly, Lex said, "I settled with Hap Haber, the way you're guessing. You claimed you had no connection with what he did to Jimmy Kemble, and I'll take that at face value. So tonight's hoedown was a private thing, too. I licked him, but he'll try again. And I don't want it used to foment other trouble."

"You mentioned a bargain."

"That's right. What I told your house-guard just now wasn't all the bluff you figured. The *Call*'s not for sale, and you can't buy it off. But if you win the election fair and square, with the people given a decent chance to make up their minds, we'll accept the situation and the *Call* will go out of business."

Palgrave's florid face could not be read. He was thinking deeply, then something caused him to shake his head.

He said, "This is Big John's last campaign — his big push. He's a sick man and knows it. He wants to beat me before he dies. I want him to die knowing that he can't do it. I don't know how much he's told you, but it runs a long ways back. To when we were both a lot younger. John and I've always argued about methods.

To this point he's been wrong every time there's been a test."

"So you're afraid to meet him in a clean fight?"

"I'm not afraid of anything."

"No, I guess not. I know about the nester war and how you got your start in politics. And I know there's more than that laying between you and Big John. The rest of us don't count, do we?"

"Not at all," Palgrave said readily.

"We'll fight your way, then," Lex said. "And be it on your head for what you're choosing." Without farewell, he turned and left.

He knew as he recrossed the town in the gathered night that in the space of a single half-day he had been carried far into deep water. He was up against a clever, ruthless, relentless man and against motives about which he knew little or nothing at all. Yet the brashness that had at last broken loose in him drove him heedlessly on.

The lamp-lighted streets of Flat Rock were filling up again, with cowhands in from the range and townsters down for a stroll or a taste of the off-street activities. The piano in the Wagonwheel was going, when Lex passed by, and its sound annoyed him. Olstein's mercantile had opened up for the evening trade. From somewhere the light, careless laughter of a woman carried to him.

He strode on toward the older part of town, where the Starlight house stood among its ageing cronies. The place was dark save for a downstairs light that Amy always left for him. He hoped that she was up, for sometimes they shared a late snack in the kitchen, and he suspected she might like to know Haber had been discouraged from laying hands on Jimmy.

But he found the lower floor empty. He paused there for a moment, feeling the room's deep peace, so sharp a contrast to the violence just behind. It was a pity it was so false for they all needed it — John, Amy, and even himself.

He blew out the lamp and ascended the stairs to his own room. It was in the front of the house, with Amy's quarters in the back end. Big John's room lay between the other two since they shared the job of attending to his needs at night. Jimmy slept by himself downstairs.

Lex stripped off his clothes in the darkness and, because the night was so hot, crawled bare-bodied into bed. He was thinking of all that the day had held, of Jimmy's experience with Haber and what had stemmed from that. The tensions of the fight loosened, leaving him sore and jaded yet still keyed to a point where he could not sleep.

Somehow his thoughts centered abruptly on Sara. She was more serious about him than he had realized, and he had to regard that as a warning. For he could very easily let go with her as he had with Haber. He wanted to; more than ever before was he tempted to light play with a woman. She was capable of responding. He knew that. Sara could let go, herself. But it took the right man, he knew now. She was neither light nor loose in her ways. What she had shown him — and there *had* been invitation in it — had been meant for him alone. His male pride rose to that, and it was also a plain male urge to conquer a spirited woman. Oddly, this reverie about her relaxed him gradually, and at last he drifted off to sleep.

He awakened with a sense of having been smashed into the bed. His head was ringing, his ears hurt and his first awareness was of crashing glass somewhere in the house. These physical reactions were sufficient to tell him that he had not dreamed it. He had heard something terrible. He shoved up on stiffened arms, trying to orient himself, staring into a shaft of moonlight that poured into his room. He grew aware that the glass was gone from the sash, that the light was heavy with stirred dust. A second later he heard something fall dully in the upstairs hall, followed by a cascading of sound. *Plaster*, he thought and sprang from the bed. *Something blew high, wide and handsome . . .*

He was too shaken to try to understand it all. He could smell the dust now and more — the acrid, hanging odor that he recognized as lingering behind exploded dynamite. His heart picked up a thumping run as he began to grasp the meaning of the situation. Then he thought of Big John with the stabbing wonder as to what this had done to that more delicate heart. He ripped a sheet from the bed, pulled it about him hastily and bolted out into the hallway.

His bare feet kicked a chunk of fallen plaster, and the dust in that closer space was chokingly thick. Amy's silence was only a little less frightening now than his concern for his father — there was no response from

42

Jimmy, downstairs. Lex nearly fell over a pile of debris before he reached Big John's door.

There he yelled, "John — you all right?"

"So far. What in hell was that?"

"Explosion of some kind."

Lex wheeled on. Amy's door was shut. He called twice and when she did not respond he put his shoulder hard against the wood. It would not give. Dread ran through him and he hit the panels once more, calling out her name. He yelled for Jimmy to fetch an axe, but there also was no response from him. Another big chunk of plaster dropped at that moment, missing him narrowly.

Big John was yelling questions and cussing when he got no answer. Reassured as to his father by that sign of vigor, Lex wheeled and raced down the stairs, his sheet streaming behind. Jimmy's room was empty, and the boy was nowhere on the lower floor. Lex ran on through the rear and out to the woodshed, hunting an axe. The back yard was filled with a litter of split boards, shingles and loose brick. There was a gaping hole in the roof, and the back chimney had disappeared entirely.

"Who?" he said aloud as he stared upward for an instant.

He had to chop down Amy's door to get into her room. He entered with raw fear running through his flesh, for this room was the closest to the exploded chimney. It was all but demolished. The window had been blown outward, furniture overturned. A whole inner wall bulged inward, split open.

Across from it, Amy's bed was collapsed. She lay half on it and half on the floor. Lex dropped to his knees and gathered her in his arms. She was small and soft and warm in this intimate touch, and he stood for an instant staring at the moonlit wreckage of the room. Then he looked down at her face and lowered his lips to her mouth, whispering, "Amy — lovely, lovely Amy . . ."

He thought that her lips stirred under his, then he carried her swiftly down the stairs and into the clean air of Jimmy's strangely vacant bedroom. He placed her on the bed there and called for the boy again. He was not surprised when there was no answer.

"Lex," Amy whispered. "What was it?"

"Dunno."

He grew aware that he had lost his sheet in the excitement. He turned and fled, climbing the stairs again. Big John still swore steadily between his yelled questions. Lex took time to pull on his pants and boots. Big John was all right and it looked like Amy had come out of it. His concern now was for Jimmy.

CHAPTER
FIVE

He grew aware of shouting in the street as the neighborhood aroused and poured forth from the houses. He heard a man yell, "Damned if I know — but it looks like something blew the roof clean off the Starlight place!" They were coming onto the porch by the time Lex got back down the stairs. He threw open the door and saw half-a-dozen figures moving across a yard that showed less litter than the rear.

"You got a still in the attic?" a man bawled senselessly.

"Somebody fetch Doc Cornell!" Lex answered. "And get the sheriff — for the little good he'll do!" A couple of men swung around to obey him.

Lex shut the door, keeping the others outside. He turned back to see Amy coming unsteadily out of the door of Jimmy's room. She rested against the door jamb for an instant.

"You all right?" he asked.

"I feel like I'd been butchered. Where's Jimmy?"

"I think somebody dropped dynamite down the kitchen chimney, Amy." He didn't want her as worried about Jimmy as he was, right then. "It goes past your room. Did you hear anything?"

She shook her head. "I just woke up and you were holding me."

Oh, Lord, he thought, *I wonder if she knows I kissed her.*

He ascended the stairs for another look at Big John. Dust hung in the air in that room but it showed no damage.

"Anybody hurt?" John asked.

"Not bad. Amy was knocked out awhile, but she's back on her feet. It was dynamite in the flue by her wall, John. I'm going to carry you downstairs where the air's fit to breathe."

"I'll walk," John growled.

"Like hell. I licked Hap Haber tonight, John. It looks like he might have tried to pay me back."

"It was Palgrave. He figured a blast like that would kill a man with my heart."

"He's not that scared of you."

"I dunno," John said. "He knows this is likely my last fight against him — that I might use all my guns. I could ruin that man in a minute if I wanted to. It was always so. Don't ask me how — that's part of our private ruckus."

Somebody was thumping up the stairs. Lex wheeled and started down, thinking some dunderhead had forced his way indoors. Then he recognized a gawky shape, highlighted by the lamp Amy had lighted below.

"Jimmy!" he gasped. "Where in the devil have you been?"

"Following the fellow!" Jimmy panted. He halted on the steps below Lex, his chest heaving. "Something

46

woke me up. I took a look out the window and seen somebody carrying our ladder back toward the woodshed. I only figured that some skunk had prowled us and was taking off. I pulled on my pants and went out the window. He'd got pretty far ahead but I could still hear him running. And I run."

"Who was it?"

"I never got close enough to see, but he was big." Jimmy swallowed hard. "Then something blew to hell and gone, but it never dawned on me that it was our house. I tailed that cuss to the gully behind Oscarson's tannery. He jumped aboard a horse there and kited it."

"Hap Haber, Jimmy?"

"Dunno — but it's likely. Coming back, I heard our house had been dynamited. That sure gave me a turn."

Big John was a load even for a man as big as Lex, who carried him down to Jimmy's bed. The old man cursed heartily at the indignity but the bedridden months had weakened him into helplessness. Doc Cornell arrived presently and could find nothing alarming in him. "You had a squeak, though," Cornell said. "But it may be a good sign. Looks like the old pump's coming along better than I hoped for. Your reward, John, for minding me. Otherwise you'd likely be dead as a mackerel right now — maybe to the good of your long-suffering physician."

"Hell," said John Starlight, "I've ridden cayuses with more jolt than that blast."

Sheriff Conbuck showed up finally, accompanied by Ferd Trapp, the slack-jawed marshal employed by the town. They asked some questions, they looked around.

"Flue gas, to my mind," Conbuck said finally. "Heard of it happening in these old rat-nest houses."

"You heard what Jimmy said about it," Lex snapped. "And you two sure gave that skunk time to get away."

A tall gaunt man with a flamboyant touch to his dress, Conbuck was middle-aged. He pulled straight and stared hard at Lex.

"Meaning on purpose?"

"Meaning just that."

"So you aim to make politics out of it, do you?"

"I aim to scalp the son of a bitch that did it, Conbuck," Lex retorted. "Politics or no, it came out of the same bunch. You're one of them. I knew that, and that you wouldn't try to catch the man. But, God help us all, you're the law till after the voting."

"That's absolutely correct," Conbuck agreed. "Except that I'll be the law after the voting, too. Jimmy Kemble only laid out a wild yarn for the public ear. Looks like he's your breed of politician, too. How come you never run him for something?" The sheriff left with the marshal, and Lex knew that was as far as the case would ever be developed.

The excitement began to subside. The crowd broke up and disappeared. The kitchen had been put out of business by the blast, but as it grew light Amy made breakfast in the fireplace, whose outside chimney was intact. Lex turned a problem in his mind. The town house was beyond living in and would be for days while repairs were being made. He was tempted, if Doc Cornell would permit it, to move John and the Kembles out to the ranch. That would be desirable if this was a sample of what lay ahead, and the only alternative was to move them to a hotel.

Lex remembered then that he had promised Holly to come out that day, anyhow, to have a look at a rustling matter. He decided to go at once and see what Holly thought about moving the family. The rustling didn't seem important at the moment but could become so if Holly and the boys opened war on Slick Ear Plateau with things already so explosive. Lex meant to get there before they would have had time to do anything.

He mentioned the move to Amy, who studied it for a moment. "I'd like to live out there, all right," she said. "I think it would be better for Jimmy, anyhow. After all, Lex, it's whatever you boys say."

"You've got a heap more say than you admit, girl," Lex told her. "I remember hearing Holly tell you so the other night."

She smiled at him, the warmest expression she had ever shown him. "I've got this to say. The next time you run around in a bedsheet, use a safety pin."

Lex felt heat crawl into his ears. "So you played possum."

The amused mystery deepened in her eyes.

"I had to come to some time, didn't I?" she asked.

Dew still clung to the grass and scattered clumps of sage when Lex topped the last rise before Toadstool's sprawled headquarters. Although Flat Rock lay less than a dozen miles in the distance, there was a sense of return, a feeling that all that was familiar and good and important to him was again at hand, that all else was alien and well put behind.

What he saw before him held beauty, though some might not have agreed. The main house was of log and stone, shaded by the poplars that Big John had set out so long ago, having imported them over a great distance because he had had a wife to protect from the sun.

Riding down upon the layout, Lex thought again of his mother. She had been a Galtry, a clan about which Big John had spoken rarely, and now Lex knew why. He kept wondering about her brother — his own uncle and Holly's — the Galtry who had gone bad. He kept wondering why Big John had kept it so close a secret, like a scandal and shame, when that could have happened to any high-spirited young fellow.

It was too deep for Lex, and he was back on Toadstool, which he had left with much private regret. He was an outdoor man, a doer more than a thinker, built for the good life of the open range and not for the quieter chores of a newspaper editor. Sometimes he hungered for physical exertion as a man might crave red meat.

He eased in the saddle, aware of the blue and cloudless sky above Toadstool, of the wheeling sweeps of its graze that ran from here to the hazed hills marking the lower edge of Slick Ear Plateau. The ranch was Big John's property now, but someday it would be the sons' to share. Lex wanted to come back here — there were few things in life that he wanted more.

Pitt Berts was at the day corral with half-a-dozen punchers, who had already saddled horses. Assigning the day's riding jobs with efficient dispatch, Pitt broke off with a smile of greeting as Lex rode into the ranchyard. Lex swung over to the corral, greeting each of the crew with a personal, friendly word. This easy manner had always made the Starlights popular with their help.

"Howdy, Sheriff," Lex said to Pitt, finally. "You building yourself a posse?"

A tall puncher made a sour face. "Hell, no. He's sending us out to blab calves while he saves the glory for himself. Turned politician, already. Won't touch a thing that don't make him look good. Lex, how come you wear your face that way? It don't become you much."

Lex grinned. "Mebbe I talked where I should have listened, Jim." They did not press the matter of his battle scars, taking his reticence as their cue to swallow their natural curiosity. A man had a right to privacy, and there were times when every man there wanted it himself. The crew rode out on the day's work.

Waiting behind, Pitt said, "Holly and me're set to ride. You had breakfast?"

"Would I come out to eat cookhouse grub when I can have Amy's?"

"No telling what a Starlight will do." Pitt frowned. "Holly's fit to be tied, this morning. I think he rowed last night with either Big John or Amy. I'd say Amy. When it's John, Holly spends the next day fuming and gets it out of his system. This morning he's got his mouth shut like a bear trap."

An uneasiness riffled in Lex as he remembered how he had crowded Holly about Amy and got a response of sudden jealousy. He thought, *The kid better grow up if he wants to get anywhere with her*. But he understood Holly better than Big John or Pitt did. Holly's small outbursts could come from other, larger issues carefully repressed and were not a good clue as to what was really eating on him.

But Lex's arrival cheered Holly and brought him out of it, if he had really been sulking. He stared at Lex's black eye and puffed mouth and failed to share the crew's reticence.

He said, "So you squared it for Jimmy."

Lex shrugged. "And doubt if I settled a thing. Somebody dynamited the house last night. Blew the roof half off and knocked Amy out cold."

Holly rocked forward, his jaw line rigid. "Haber did it?"

"I'd guess so," Lex admitted, and he told them about it.

"Let's go find Haber," Holly said hotly. "The hell with the rustlers. That lousy bastard might have killed Big John and Amy both."

"You're right, there," Lex agreed. "But we won't go after him just yet. Big John thinks it was more than Haber's spite work because of that fight. He says Palgrave figured a shock would kill him and that's what it was aimed at. There's something secret between them two, Holly. John told me as much, last night. But he clammed up tight as to what it was."

"Then let's go string up some rustlers," Holly said. "And maybe I'll feel better."

Their horses stood at the yard hitch rail, waiting. While Pitt and Holly walked over to get them, Lex went into the house for his own shell belt and sixgun. The old house, worn and cluttered from the long years of baching, was a pleasanter place to him than the town place could ever be. The gun felt good on his hip. He looked at his hands, hungry for the day when they would again feel a saddle rope rather than cold type and printer's ink.

When he went outdoors again, the other two men were set to ride.

"That rustling was another Palgrave beef issue, Lex," Holly said as they started out.

"Beef issue?"

"You heard me. The first one in years, and another sign that you've thrown a scare into Palgrave. It's been a long time since he figured it necessary to court the nesters with free beef. He's trying to offset the headway Big John made in Kinsey Flats by running Tom Lerner for a county job."

"I'll be jiggered," Lex said. "What makes you figure it that way, Holly?"

"Only way it can be figured. Pitt and me had no trouble riding the sign. Four men made a cut on the beef we've been grazing on the south slope. They tried a couple of times to foul trail but weren't very good at it. They pulled a sandy to make it look like they'd headed up the river to go out through the gorge."

"You had a different opinion?"

Holly grinned. "The sheriff, there. Pitt smelled a rat. We circled and picked up sign again and sure enough. It followed the edge of Slick Ear Plateau all the way to Kinsey Flats. By now them steers have gone into nester bellies and jars and jerky. Just like in the old days that John used to talk about. A lot of nesters who might have voted for Lerner have changed their minds. Lerner's a nester but he's honest. He wouldn't give 'em any rustled free beef."

Lex's countenance had turned black. In the early years the nesters had nearly starved on the land they were trying to break to the plow. The law had been curiously inactive about the rustling that went on steadily, some of it so open there could be no mistaking who was guilty. Yet Conbuck, who had held office concurrently with Palgrave, had been as dilatory in his investigations as he had been quick to punish reprisals by the cowmen. Election years had been particularly bad, and such raids had come to be called the Palgrave beef issue.

But there was now no question of the nesters needing food. As a class they were the most prosperous people in the country. A beef issue at this time could only serve to remind them of their indebtedness to Palgrave, his ability and willingness to bend the law in their favor. So Holly seemed to have guessed correctly. The surprise in this campaign had been Big John's ability to persuade a man influential among the nesters to run on the opposition ticket.

Pitt Berts said, "Well, we won't get anywhere riding onto the flats with blood in our eye. Them squatters learned how to hide evidence way back. Anyhow, Conbuck would opine that the rustlers tried to throw suspicion their way or even that we planted the sign to make a political stink."

"You're picking up real political savvy," Lex commented. "That's what he accused me of doing, last night. But I'd like to ride that sign. It might make a story for the paper."

They were on an easterly course. The old familiar country, with its dry grass and simmering rims, was a tonic to Lex. The saddle felt good beneath him. Maybe this was a break, the makings of the hardest punch he had yet been able to throw at Palgrave through the *Call*. Nothing would stir the cattle basin as strongly as word of another beef issue. Even among the nesters there were upright men, like Tom Lerner, who would not have been cut in on this new Palgrave generosity. They would not take kindly to such a thing. Maybe Palgrave's cynical maneuver had been his first major blunder in this campaign.

Below Pilot Rock, Holly showed Lex where he had picked up sign. It was open country until they came to Crinkle Creek, where a clumsy effort had been made to foul trail. This happened again at a long patch of shale the rustlers had sought out deliberately. In neither case would a good tracker have been held up long. Thereafter the trail used by the outlaws had angled northeast toward a distant break in the rim.

"No need to waste energy smelling it on out," Holly said. "We're bound to pick it up again south of here."

He pointed the way until they were again on the trail. The sign led boldly south, after that, the rustlers confident that they had been misleading enough to escape detection. Two hours later the three cattlemen were on the high rim that made a clean break between

Kinsey Flats and the roughs that separated the flats from Starlight Basin. They could see plainly where the stolen cattle had been driven down onto the level to vanish into the heat-hazed distance.

"Want to follow it to the end and risk gun trouble?" Holly asked, his affirmative desire showing plainly on his face.

"More tracks is all we'd find," Pitt said. "They've had time to hide everything else."

Lex agreed with Pitt. "We won't be fools enough to make charges, boys. I'll just put it in the paper. A story about rustling on Toadstool and an account of where the tracks led. That would go a sight farther toward turning out the vote than trying to jail a few nesters would. If Palgrave's behind this, we've got to make it backfire in his face."

They sat their saddles for a long while, smoking and talking it over. If this was Hap Haber's work, Lex reflected, the man was even more deadly an enemy than it had appeared. The rustling would have been in his mind, already accomplished, when he made his blustering threats to Jimmy after beating the boy up. So all the other developments had stemmed from that incident on the river bridge.

Finally Lex said, "Let's go home, boys. I've seen all I need."

CHAPTER
SIX

They swung their horses and started to retrace their course. They had gone but a short way when Pitt, in sudden alertness, pulled straight in the saddle. He stared hard into the forward distance, saying, "Boys, somebody tailed us. I swear I seen a horse cut out of sight up ahead."

The country they were now re-entering was rough and sun-splashed so that visibility was poor. Lex could see nothing up there, and even Holly looked passive.

"Lex," Pitt said, "do you reckon Haber could have seen you pull out of town this morning?"

Lex shrugged. "If he was in town. It's more likely that somebody seen you and Pitt ride the sign, yesterday, and has been watching to see what comes of it. Whoever it is, if you really seen somebody, he's high-tailed it."

"I seen him, and he's high-tailed it. We better watch our step."

The trail fell away and presently it became necessary to enter the roughs. All three men kept a hand close to their guns, their eyes shifting keenly across the forward area. Lex still could see nothing alarming but respected Pitt's feeling. That keenness of sense had prompted Big

John to pick him as candidate for sheriff. Presently they came upon plain evidence of a horse moving down from the rim to pound ahead on the main trail.

"Well, we scared him worse than he did us," Holly said.

His words were echoed by the crack of a rifle that was loud in the enfolding quiet. Lex's hat left his head as he bent forward in quick instinct, driving home his spurs. The others followed his example, bewildered, their startled horses streaking forward, all of them still exposed to a commanding position on the rim. The rifle fired again and again, angrily persistent, the slugs narrowly missing the swift-moving marks. The riders swept on into a cluster of pinnacle rocks, where they pulled down with drawn guns.

"That was a purty one," Pitt breathed. "One cuss lit out to draw us in where the other waited to bushwhack us. The only way up to the reptile is the way the first come down. We'd be shot dead before we got halfway up there."

"We've got a better chance to catch the one on the cayuse!" Holly yelled. "Let's try it!"

They went forward at a driving clip, although the trail grew rougher. The tracks of the flogged horse ahead of them were easy to discern and follow. The rider knew that part of the ambushed party might get through and pursue him. The country was too tumbled in here for him to try anything but a headlong flight.

The Toadstool horses were tough, work-hardened, but the one Lex kept in town had grown soft enough to fall a little behind. Pitt and Holly pulled ahead, knowing that if they could nail their quarry they would have something embarrassing to Sheriff Conbuck. The most crooked of law officers could not brush off too many responsibilities. Presently Lex's companions were lost to him in the forward breaks.

Knowing he was out of the chase, Lex let his punished horse slow down. He was thinking of his hat, which he had not dared to retrieve. A sudden, overriding temptation rose in him to go back and get it. There was a good chance that he might surprise the actual ambusher and put another twist in Conbuck's tail.

He had gone but a short distance on the back trail when he grew aware of oncoming horses. He pulled down hastily, listened a moment, then cut off in a short swing to his left. A rock scab lay over there, and he gigged his horse, fearing he would not have time to make cover. Concealed in the cluster, a moment later, he swung down and went to the head of his horse to keep it quiet while the others passed. He had barely done it when a party of three riders whipped into view on the back trail. They were coming fast, determined to lend help to the man Pitt and Holly were after.

Lex's breath nearly stopped as they thundered past his hiding place. There was a shock in actually seeing Hap Haber, leading a couple of toughs who raised stock on Slick Ear Plateau, even though Lex had suspected the man's part in this from the start. But a settled feeling followed. He was sure now, which would make for easier going. He let them get on a distance before he swung back into the saddle.

He rode cautiously behind them, fearing they would surprise Pitt and Holly. He meant to deliver a surprise, himself, if that happened, with the outlaws on the receiving end. After he had kept up his stealthy pursuit for some ten minutes he grew aware that the sound of other travel had faded out. Those ahead could have outdistanced him or they could have halted. He doubled his caution. They were on the basin side of the roughs, now, with the country flattening and straightening out. This was not a regular thoroughfare but recent travel had scuffed up a well-defined trail.

Presently a brightness on the trail caused Lex to pull down hastily. It was a dropped knife, open-bladed and glittering, a skinning knife. Partly covered by dust kicked up by a fast-moving horse, it lay in the middle of the trail. Lex swung down. Picking up the knife, he was certain that it belonged to himself. He stroked his jaw, his mind stilled by its sheer astonishment. There were hundreds of skinning knives in the country, but this one bore the Toadstool arched-T brand, scratched on the blade close to the guard. A nick had been filed out of the blade and Lex remembered doing that long ago.

His puzzlement came from the fact that for a long while he had used the knife as a letter opener at the *Call* shop and had not even missed it. On the range such knives — used in salvaging the hides of dead steers — were carried in scabbards. It was next to impossible for one to bounce loose and be lost. It was probable that this one had been planted here by the riders just passed, none of them aware that a man had dropped behind them.

Why? Hap Haber knew the answer to that and probably bigger men than Haber understood it even better.

Lex straightened, again listening intently. In the complete stillness resulting from his own inaction, he could hear the distant crackle of gunfire. It was well ahead and just breaking out. He swung into saddle and drove home his spurs once more.

Dropping onto the floor of the last canyon, he stopped the horse. Spaced shooting punctured the lonely quietude, ahead and on this immediate reach of the trail. He didn't need to be told that Pitt and Holly had been stopped and pinned down. Probably the man they chased had turned on them, confident of help coming from behind. Lex left his horse, checked his gun and started forward afoot. He picked his way through the rocks of the left talus, helped by the concealing shadows of the high cliffs.

As he went on, he worked his way higher onto the slope for he was powerless until he located his allies as well as his foes. But the spaced, determined shooting was telling him much. He worked along through the shade so quietly that he drew no fire himself.

He was sure that the Toadstool riders were nailed down on the exposed canyon floor, a man ahead potting at them to keep them there. He knew that they had been surprised from behind by Haber's appearance with the Slick Ear gunfighters. It was Haber and company that Lex wanted to catch unawares.

He halted dead still when he saw an exposed leg just below him. The full figure was lost among the low-lying rocks but the general situation convinced him that it was one of the enemy. His gun clutched in a steady hand, he moved down a little. He saw more of his man's back but still not enough that he was willing to drive in a shot. Edging farther to the right, he rose slightly and then sent in a bullet.

He moved in fast, afterward, crossing the open space and landing on the man he had shot at. But his slug had angled in from an elevation and drilled through the man's back. The fellow lay still, his cheek relaxed against the saddle carbine he had used. In his spring, Lex had pulled out the skinning knife he had found on the trail, but now he slid it back under his belt.

He lay motionless, breathing quietly, ignoring the dead ex-resident of the outlaw plateau. The crack of his pistol, at this angle, had notified the others that a change had taken place. The whole canyon became still. Looking along the barrel of the dead man's carbine, Lex located the floor-littering rocks that probably hid Holly and Pitt. He could not see his allies. He had seen nothing of horses, either, but the animals had been dismounted abruptly at the fight's eruption and would have thundered on along the trail.

Lex heard movement, soft and slithering, like that of a giant reptile. He swung his head. A shot hammered into the stillness. He fired at the powder flash, faintly seen in the shaded area on the talus. The shots resounded back and forth in the canyon, a bitter exchange. He wanted to yell and identify himself to his comrades but had to trust they could guess as well as Haber could.

He spotted a man high on the right slope, hidden behind a rock segment that had tumbled down from the high cliff. The bright sunlight struck the spot and he saw the momentary glint of a gun barrel. He waited through the tense seconds for a head to appear. But the man lost his nerve. Lex began to work backward, meaning to circle and get in above him. A bullet glanced off the rock above him and threw splinters in his face. He heard another shot pound out behind and crawled back to where he had been before, himself as badly pinned down now as were Pitt and Holly.

He cursed silently, informed that Haber had divided the bottom and two slopes among himself and the men who had helped him attack from the rear. Haber and another had the commanding positions here, and the man whose flight had baited the trap had plugged up the way ahead. The Toadstool men had to win to live.

Haber's making hay where he finds it, Lex thought, *or we blundered into something we weren't smart enough to foresee . . .*

The quiet of a tense, deadly gunfight came on again. He became aware of vibrations in the earth before he heard the sound of massed hoofs in the distance. A wild relief surged up in him, though he had not yet discerned the direction — the hope that it was some of the Toadstool crew somehow grown suspicious. Then he realized that the riders were coming in from the other direction. If it was help at all, it came from Slick Ear Plateau, and his elation died.

If it was help for Haber, it did not energize the man into an outburst of renewed action. Except for the loudening drum of hoofs, the silence ran on. The horsemen whipped in boldly, but Lex did not dare to rise up enough to take a look. Yet Haber could see from his elevation and was not shooting at them.

A voice bawled, "What the hell is going on here?" and it was the voice of Sheriff Conbuck.

"Watch yourselves, boys!" Haber called from the talus. "We got them Starlight roosters and Pitt Berts! Caught 'em red-handed at their stinking tricks and they showed fight!"

"Stand up without your guns!" Conbuck yelled back. "The lot of you till I get this sorted out!"

Lex's mind was numb. The thing looked rehearsed, carefully studied out, particularly the way Conbuck had ridden in so boldly on a gun battle. It was as if they had understood the situation and known that the only ones in a position to shoot at them would not do so. That was not surprising. Haber and Conbuck — outlaw and sheriff — worked for one and the same man.

Haber shoved up boldly in his place on the talus. The heavy face, which Lex's fist had battered, now showed a confident grin. Another man appeared on the opposite slope. Angrily Lex dropped his gun, as ordered, and rose to take a look at the newcomers.

He blinked his eyes. Conbuck sat his horse in a line that had spread across the narrow canyon, half-a-dozen men with drawn guns. The highly polished star on his vest glittered in the bright sunlight, a false, cynical symbol of law and order. He was trying to look stern, judicious, but actually he appeared pleased.

The man on the horse next to the sheriff interested Lex the more. It was Tom Lerner, the nester running for office against the machine, Big John's candidate for Renwick's seat on the county commission. Lerner caught Lex's stare and returned it angrily, his ageing, high-boned face brown and bleak.

The third man's presence was equally surprising, considering the circumstances. Staff Palgrave, smoking a cigar in a strange kind of savor, had his political smile on his face. He was eyeing Tom Lerner, weighing the effect of this situation on the nester leader. That unguarded inspection gave Lex his first inkling as to the meaning of the set-up. They were trying to drive a wedge between Lerner and the cattlemen he had thrown in with for the coming campaign.

Switching his attention to Lex, Palgrave said, "I'm surprised at you. Wasn't it just last night that you lectured me on political ethics?"

Ignoring him, Lex looked at the nester, saying, "What you doing in this kind of company, Tom?"

Lerner shifted his weight in the saddle and maintained an utter silence.

Conbuck was looking beyond Lex, who turned then to see that Holly and Pitt had risen at the spot where he had figured them to be. He was relieved that they looked unhurt. Farther down stood the man who had pinned them there. "Now," Conbuck said to them generally, "supposing somebody explains this shindig."

Lex knew better than to say anything until he had heard how Haber meant to account for it. From their sullen silence, Holly and Pitt appeared to see it the same way.

With no such reticence, Hap Haber said, "Yesterday me and the boys seen Berts and Holly Starlight drive a cut of beef onto Kinsey Flats. Don't know what they done with 'em, but pretty soon they come back and weren't driving a damned thing. Now there's never been a market for Toadstool beef on the flats. It looked real curious. We kept watch, and bedamned if they didn't come back today with Lex along. We tried to stop 'em and ask some questions. They gave us a fight."

Conbuck had turned his attention to Tom Lerner. It was typical of his law enforcement that he was not curious to hear the other side. He said, "Well, Tom, it's what we figured, ain't it? They tried to plant rustling evidence on you nesters."

"That's what you figured," Lerner growled. "I never offered an opinion."

In a gentle voice, Lex said, "Tom, this might make sense if you'd tell us what's got you so riled."

Lerner's eyes met Lex's and were as cold and shocking as a blast of blizzard wind.

"Starlight," he said, "I admired the kind of campaigns Big John always run. But when you take over you get dirty. You made headway for a while with some of us nesters. But this stinking trick has sure wiped it out."

"Get down to brass tacks, Tom," Lex returned. "I haven't the slightest notion of what you're talking about."

"Oh no? Haber tipped me off to what he'd seen going on in here. I trailed them planted steers to Parson's Sink, where they had been beefed and skinned and their carcasses sunk in the quicksand. Your brother and Berts scattered the hides around to pin the deadwood on the nester colony. That's an old sore, Starlight — one you'd best have left alone. I'm withdrawing my name from your slate."

"So they fed it to you, hook, line and sinker," Lex breathed.

And in that moment he saw the most cherished dreams of his father fall into ruins. The shock of realizing Tom Lerner's final and total acceptance of their version of the situation must have shown in Lex's face, for Palgrave smiled to himself. Conbuck looked easy, a travesty on law and justice. Haber was grinning broadly, too obtuse to know that it betrayed him.

"Tom!" Holly yelled. "You're too smart to swallow that! Why didn't you come to us, man? Why turn to Conbuck and his lousy law?"

"I sent for the sheriff," Lerner said, "because I wanted the facts on record. Somebody's planted green Toadstool hides on us, and I wanted to be the first to report it. Conbuck built the theory. I kept an open mind, but this shindig here sure seems to bear him out."

"Maybe you think you see through it," Lex blazed. "But that's more than I do! We want all the nesters we can get on our side. Why would we try to offend or frame them? Tell me that, and maybe I can credit you with good sense."

"I explained that to Tom," Palgrave cut in. "You meant to call it one of those old beef issues. You figured it would destroy what little support I have with the cowmen. You planted the hides on nesters who would have voted for me, anyhow. You expected the rest to rise up in wrath along with Tom. But he was too smart for you."

"What are you along for, anyhow, Palgrave?" Pitt drawled. "The ride?"

"Conbuck told me Tom had sent for him and why," Palgrave returned readily. "And I think I've got a stake in it, myself." The man was relaxed, confident. He had gained what he wanted, which was Lerner's withdrawal from the contest for political office.

Lerner was highly offended and resentful, apparently unable to think with detachment. He sat his plug horse on the hot canyon floor, his thin shoulders hunched. Pride in his kind was high in him, and he felt that his whole breed had been wronged.

Hap Haber came down the slope. At a point above Lex, he halted and stared down in sudden interest. He had discovered the outlaw that Lex had shot, the body concealed until then in the low-lying rocks.

"It's not only politics, boys," he yelled. "It's murder. Conbuck, come take a look at a dead man. I wondered where Lefty Farnol went. Killing a man while committing a crime is murder, ain't it, Conbuck?"

"It sure is," Conbuck said. He sounded excited all over again.

Palgrave also showed a quickened interest. He took the cigar from his lips and straightened in the saddle so he could see. Conbuck moved his horse forward, his face turned tight and thoughtful. He saw the dead Slick Ear outlaw behind Lex. For a long moment he studied the unmoving figure. Then he looked at Lex.

"What have you got to say about that?" he demanded. He was pleased, already extending his plans. For a moment he and Palgrave exchanged a private glance.

Ignoring them, Lex turned toward Lerner. "Tom, if you're the man I figured, you haven't got much use for Conbuck and none at all for Haber and his Slick Ear cronies. They knew where to jab you to get you mad. In your pride in the colony. You can make or break the machine, depending on what you do now. They're playing you for a sucker. They figured you'd be stupid enough to take bait and pull out of the fight. Don't hand it to them that easy."

Conbuck's voice punched out. "Shut up, Starlight! You're caught red-handed and the three of you will face a murder charge!"

Lerner stared at the sheriff through an extended moment. Slowly he said, "Conbuck, if you want to look at a fool, get yourself a mirror. It seemed funny to me that you never let them speak their piece but played pattycake with Haber. Starlight's right about that man — I don't trust him any. Now you're jumpin' to the son's suggestion that you make a murder case outta this. That's some serious. After that, I reckon I'll hear Starlight's side of the story."

"Thanks," Lex breathed. "This is what really happened. Yesterday Pitt and Holly found that a cut of our steers had been run off our east slope. They didn't have much trouble tracking it to the edge of the nester flats. I saw the boys in town, yesterday evening, and they told me. This morning we set out to take a better look. We stopped at the edge of the flats because we didn't want to brush with you nesters. But we should have gone on. This whole deal is Palgrave's frame-up, and it worked even better than he hoped. We dealt them a hand of aces when we rode the sign again this morning."

"It's warm enough in this blasted canyon," Conbuck drawled, "without all that hot air."

The leathery face of Tom Lerner showed new concern. A dogged look came into it as he tried stubbornly to pick the thing apart, saying, "Now, you wait a minute, Conbuck. You and Palgrave were some anxious to have me ride this trail with you, this morning. We'd go over to Toadstool, you said, and get to the bottom of it. Well, coming over this trail, it struck me that you kept looking for something. Finally you found a man's hat."

"But he wasn't looking for a hat, Tom," Lex cut in quickly. "What he hunted was a skinning knife Haber planted on the trail to make it look like we'd been over it. The reason Conbuck never found it is that I did." He touched the knife in his belt and saw the flick of a shadow on Conbuck's face. "And the hat he found was mine."

"How'd you lose it?" Lerner asked sharply.

"Somebody tried to dry gulch us. That jigger down the canyon decoyed us into it, and then on into this gun trap. It was rigged for a deadfall, Tom. We never had a chance."

"There's no liar like a caught one, Tom," Palgrave drawled.

"Something's mighty fishy," Lerner said, and flung a sudden look at the politician. "If you've played me for a numskull, Palgrave . . ."

"Now, Tom!" Palgrave said hastily, "don't let them mix you up! We've learned what we wanted to know, and there's no need to go on to Toadstool. I'll ride home with you."

"Reckon I'll ride alone," Lerner said. He swung his horse and rode off, a confused and uncertain man but at least on the fence.

"You boys crowded your luck too hard," Lex said grimly. "You had him till you tried to work this thing for all there is in it. Now you're worried again. I hope it makes you think twice before you crowd it any farther. Conbuck, am I under arrest?"

The sheriff shook his head. "Not till this has gone before a grand jury. I ain't giving the basin a rallying point in you. Just the same, one of you beefed Lefty Farnol, and I say the circumstances make it murder."

"You've pulled in your horns a lot since Tom Lerner started to show sense."

"You know, Lex," Palgrave said, "we could save everybody a lot of trouble."

"Now it comes. What's your price?"

The man smiled. "And when I offer a bargain, I try to make it more attractive than the one you offered me last night. It looks like we're checkmated on Tom

Lerner at the moment. Let's let it stay that way — him pulling out of the race with that block of nester votes he controls."

"Or be railroaded," Lex asked softly, "by a crooked county machine?"

"You boys just think it over."

Conbuck spoke gruffly to his deputies. "You shytpokes scare up these jiggers' horses. I'm letting 'em all go — free men for a while."

Two of the deputies rode out. Lex had no reply to make to Palgrave, nor did the man expect one just then. Lex moved down to Pitt and Holly and saw the shocked animosity on their faces. Steeled as he was against showing uncertainty before his enemies, Lex shared his saddle-mates' deep uneasiness. The machine was skilled at expediency. Haber and Conbuck had made much of this day's opportunities, serving Palgrave well. There was no doubt that the situation would be squeezed until the machine had gained every last drop of advantage.

Lex swung his attention to the elated Haber, remembering the dynamited house. It dawned on him that he dared not accuse the man outright of being responsible. Haber might already realize that Jimmy had trailed him through town after the explosives were planted and the fuse ignited. The boy could get into trouble enough without having Haber after him again.

At last the deputies came back, leading the escaped horses. Lex walked to Conbuck and said, "I'll take my hat. It was more damaging to you than to me, the way Lerner saw it. And a man needs a hat in the sun."

Actually he was afraid of some distorted use Conbuck might make of it. But the man had been rendered uncertain, and he handed it over. Then Palgrave rode off, heading back toward the nester flats, his henchmen following obediently. Lefty Farnol's body was lashed carelessly across a saddle.

CHAPTER
SEVEN

For a moment the Toadstool riders stood in their tracks. Pitt Berts' face was dark.

"I never much wanted the sheriff's job," he said. "To tell you the truth, I was hoping I wouldn't draw many votes. But when I stood here and heard a man behind a law badge talk the way Conbuck did, I went sicker than a scoured steer. Me, I think I'm going to get out and politick for that office."

"They meant business with that offer," Holly reflected. "The Lefty Farnol thing won't stay fresh very long. Lex as good as admitted he was the one who shot Farnol. If he don't pull his punches he's apt to be in jail real soon — you and me with him as accomplices."

"Then let's go to jail," Pitt said promptly. He pulled up his thick shoulders, and Lex had never seen him so moved. Maybe Palgrave had succeeded in getting one opposition candidate to withdraw from the race, but in Pitt Berts he had created a new and stubborn one.

They rode home, grim men, tired and jaded after the long hours of strain. When they reached Toadstool, Holly got out a bottle of whisky and passed it around, a practice to which none of them was much addicted.

Then they took seat on the shaded porch to make their own medicine.

"From here on," Pitt said, "it hinges on who run the steers onto the flats, who jumped who in the roughs today, and whether Lex murdered Lefty Farnol or shot him in self-defense."

"And whether or not Tom Lerner pulls out on us," Lex added. "He's a slow thinker, but when he makes up his mind it stays made up. Palgrave knows that."

"Well," Pitt said, "there's still another block of votes Palgrave figures is in his hat, which we ain't thought much about. The stockmen on Slick Ear. A mighty fine thing for this country would be to have it cleaned out for good and all. It would knock out a piece of Palgrave's margin, to boot."

"That's right," Holly agreed. "We don't have to swing too many votes our way. That's why Lerner was so important to Palgrave. Clean out Slick Ear, and there wouldn't be any way he could recover what he lost there."

"Wait a minute, boys," Lex said. "What you're talking about means gun trouble."

"What's wrong with that?" Holly demanded. "I kind of liked the taste of what we had back there."

"You know what Big John would say about you taking Toadstool into war on Slick Ear." Knowing how dangerous their thoughts were growing, Lex decided to change the subject completely. He said, "And that reminds me. The town house is sure a mess and no place for John and Amy. What do you think about moving them out here, Holly — anyhow until after the election?"

Holly grinned sourly. "You got to be told what I think about it? But try to get Amy to move out here after the row we had last night. She chewed me good."

"What about?"

"You and me — and her."

"How do I cut in on it?"

"As the man on hand," Holly drawled. "Which seems to be worth two on the range to a woman."

Lex shoved to his feet, frowning. "You're crazy. I've never got to first base with Amy."

"So? Well, you were pointed out to me last night as an example I'd be smart to follow."

"Then she don't know me as well as I do."

"Maybe you don't know Amy as well as I do," Holly returned. "Anyhow, I didn't like that, having heard it all my life from Big John. I don't happen to be you, and I don't happen to want to be."

Lex made himself laugh at that, although it stung. He said, "Look, kid — it's no time for us to row over a girl, especially when it looks as if she don't want either of us. You idiot, you're too light and easy with her. Did you ever go at her seriously?"

"Started out to last night and got brought up short."

"So you quit joking about her marrying you, all at once, and expected her to jump right into your lap. You knothead, you'll have some serious courting to do before Amy'll know for sure that you mean it."

Holly's face had a sudden troubled look that was almost boyish. "I'll be damned if I can come right out and tell her how I feel."

"False pride," Pitt snorted. "You're scared to hand a woman your heart because you're scared she'll laugh at it." He rose and walked off, embarrassed by the turn of the talk.

"Maybe he's right," Holly said, "but that don't change a thing. Maybe I was cagey when I tried to feel her out, last night. But there was nothing uncertain about the way she turned me down." He looked at his brother sharply. "What makes you so sure she's thrown you out with the potato peelings? It didn't strike me so, the way she talked about you last night."

An odd feeling was beginning to stir in Lex. *I wonder if she's played us against each other?* he thought. *Who'd ever suspect that in little Amy?* Yet she apparently realized he had kissed her, after the explosion, and she had not appeared to have been displeased by the recollection, afterward.

Abruptly, he said, "How'd it hit you if it was me she married, then?"

Holly shrugged. "Dunno. You're the two people I care the most about. I'd sure like to see you both happy. But I'd hate like hell to have to watch you living together."

When he had watered his horse and had coffee at the cookhouse, Lex left for Flat Rock. Holly and Pitt had turned quiet, too quiet, and he knew they were really interested in taking the crew to Slick Ear after Hap Haber and his cronies. Lex was tempted, himself, but he realized there could be no surer way of blowing the lid off the whole county.

It was by then past noon, and he had the sun due ahead of him. He pulled his hat brim over his eyes and let his horse set its own pace. He realized belatedly that he and Holly had reached no decision about moving the family to Toadstool. Now he did not want Amy to go, not ever.

When he reached town he left his horse at Jenkins' livery. The stableman stared at him, then said, "You punch that hole in your hat to air your brains?"

"They need it sometimes," Lex said. He offered no explanation.

Jenkins' curiosity was high and bald. "I've been worrying about you all day. Haber, he got his cayuse and rode out of town right behind you, this morning. I was scared he meant to tail you — and he did. You kill the varmint?"

"Haber and me settled our differences last night, Trink."

"The hell you say. Nobody ever settled anything with that curly-wolf because nobody's killed him yet. You think it was him who dropped dynamite down your chimney?"

Lex shrugged and walked away.

Sara was still at the *Call* office. She looked up from her work with surprise when she saw Lex come in. It was not only his bullet-drilled hat that aroused her, but the marks on his face remaining from the fist fight with Hap Haber. She might not have heard about that, Trink

Jenkins being the only witness. But she must have heard all about the explosion.

"Lex!" she cried. "The things that happen, once you get started!"

Her faint mockery puzzled him, for it was not devoid of sympathy. When her gaze lingered on his beltline, he understood another thing that had stirred not only her curiosity but Jenkins', the skinning knife he carried. He drew it out and placed it in his desk drawer, saying nothing of his own puzzlement about how it had got out of here to appear so mysteriously in the breaks.

Sara had puzzled him many times, but no one could mistake her pure dislike of the political situation, her desire to see crookedness and corruption cleaned out of the town and county. Thinking of this, he realized that her animosity seemed to turn about Hap Haber. He remembered that she had said Haber came to her house, that if he caught her alone there she feared he would give her trouble. Yet Lex was wary of her, suddenly, although he could not have said why he felt that way.

When he neglected to explain the knife, Sara said, "Well, I'm glad you're still in one piece. You frightened me for a moment. You've had serious trouble."

"Thought you liked a fireball."

"Would that keep me from worrying about him?"

"You crowd a man to fight so you can worry about him, do you?"

She had come to stand by his desk, where he had seated himself. On impulse she dropped a hand over his. She let it rest there, and the hand was at once a limp and lively thing. She met his glance, smiled and squeezed his hand, and in that small action something leaped between them that reminded him of his resolve to go easy with this girl.

"I wasn't crowding you to fight, exactly. I was only trying to help you be your own man."

He grinned. "You're discerning."

"Yes — and built like you. I've got to lead my own life."

She withdrew her hand, and he watched her walk away from him, a slim, lithe figure so capable of stirring a man and yet somehow insulated so that he could not understand her fully. He said, "You're the strangest woman I ever met. Some ways you're more like a man. I made a bad job of saying it the other day when I offended you. What I mean is, you're built like me in more than the need to be your own boss."

She knew he was trying to get at things she preferred to keep hidden, but a look of sharpening interest came onto her face. "How do you mean?"

He laughed. "Not physically but still of the flesh, if you can unscramble that. Your emotions — the run of your mind, you've got needs like a man's got them. Haven't you?"

"Maybe. But not the liberties of a man."

"Well, you let a man see that a little, and he likes it. That's why I've been bolder, I guess, than I should have been. I'm sorry I sounded like I was making light of you, the other evening. I just don't feel a need to talk in circles with you, Sara."

80

"You're talking in one now. You're trying to find out how far I'd go with you."

He could feel the heat spread on his face. Yet her eyes crinkled and he had to laugh with her. She was dead right. He was like Holly, afraid to venture too much with a woman until he was sure of her.

"Damned if I'll ask outright."

"And damned if I'll answer any way at all." Sara got her purse and left and did not look displeased by the turn of the conversation.

Presently Lex got up and walked out, locking the door behind him. He had grown aware of a duality of mind, a conflict of desires that puzzled him and was a little disturbing. He was certain now that she was playing for keeps. But that knowledge, and his respect for it, did not lessen his desire to possess her in the lighter way he still wanted. And he sensed that she would accept that way if it was the only one possible.

As he neared the Starlight house, he could hear sawing and hammering. He hurried on, surprised and curious. The litter, he discovered, had been cleared from the yard all about the house. A staging had appeared on the damaged roof, with a scaffold running along the wall below. At least a dozen men were up there, swarming about, passing boards, fitting, sawing, and nailing them down. There was more new lumber in the yard, with a stack of bundled shingles, and there was a white-rimmed box where somebody had mixed a batch of mortar.

Lex stopped in the yard, his hands on his hips, to yell, "What in hell's going on here?"

A man on the scaffold turned around. He had a hammer in his hand and took some nails from between his lips. It was Ray Mill, a bartender at the Wagonwheel. Lex recognized the hardware man, also, and the town's regular carpenter who apparently was bossing the job.

Mill grinned down at Lex. "Why, son, we're nailing fins on your house for you. Next time, she can take off like a rocket."

Amy had appeared at the door below and was smiling. Lex went on into the house. She had a cloth about her head, and he realized that she had spent the whole day cleaning the interior. The downstairs showed no sign of the night's violence.

"Who set it going?" he asked.

"It was spontaneous, I guess," Amy said happily. "The carpenter and bricklayer showed up right after you left, this morning. Before I knew it there was a wagon here with lumber and shingles and brick. Then all kinds of men arrived. They swore they'd have the house better than it ever was by dark, and it looks like they'll make it."

Lex swallowed hard. "I'll be jiggered — they did it for Big John."

"Of course. If Palgrave was behind the dynamiting he knows two things he didn't before. Big John's a hard man to kill, and he's got a lot of friends in this country."

He looked in on John, but the old man was asleep in spite of the racket and there was the ghost of a smile on his face. Lex closed the door gently and went upstairs to get another hat, his present one having aroused too much interest.

The plaster had been cleaned away up there, the furniture had been removed from Amy's shattered bedroom and piled in John's. The sprung wall in Amy's room had been torn out. The brickmason was finishing the new flue, and he gave Lex a half scowl, not wanting any show of gratitude. Lex grinned at him and let it go at that for the time being.

He found that, thanks to Amy again, his own room was fresh and neat. He thought, *She'll have to take this one for a while. Jimmy and me can sleep in the old carriage house.* The thought of her using his bed was pleasant, yet it struck up a curiosity in him as well. Never in his association with her had he felt the wild flame of physical need that he felt when he even thought of Sara. Amy Kemble lived on a plane of her own.

CHAPTER
EIGHT

Lex went down the stairs again and found Amy in the kitchen. It had been cleaned of the chimney soot that had been blown everywhere by the blast. She was busy replacing things on the shelves. She smiled but did not stop her work for him.

After a moment she said, "Maybe for Jimmy's sake we should have moved out to the ranch. Lex, he really scares me. He bears a hatred of Hap Haber that's too big for a boy his age."

"For a private reason?" Lex asked, suspecting that she knew more than she had divulged.

She seemed to consider for a moment whether she should answer that. Then she said, "He thinks Haber is the one who killed Dad. When Jimmy first mentioned that suspicion, I made him promise never to say anything to anybody else. Whether he's right or wrong, he'd get killed if Haber knew he was talking like that. And I'm not sure that Haber doesn't suspect it."

Lex rolled a cigarette and stared at her thoughtfully. "Mind saying what Jimmy bases that notion on?"

"When we lived on the spread," Amy said, "Jimmy always worked with Dad and knew things I didn't. We had rustling, the way everybody in the basin had it, except that we came so close to going broke we couldn't let it go on. You remember that. Dad took to watching things at night. One night he drove off some rustlers. He didn't tell Jimmy what he saw. I expect that was because of Jimmy's way of taking things into his own hands. But the next time Dad saw Haber, he told him not to try it again. Jimmy was there and heard that. You know what happened a couple of nights later. Dad was shot down on the range. Our herd was taken, and Jimmy and I were left without a thing."

"I knew most of that," Lex said, his face darkening. "Except that warning to Haber. If I was Jimmy, I'd think just what he does. But I don't think you need to worry about his watching his tongue. He does. I'm about as close a friend as he has, and he's never told me about that threat."

Yet Amy did not seem greatly reassured, saying, "I was afraid even to tell Conbuck how Dad had warned Haber. It seemed to me as bad as bracing Haber himself. Conbuck would only have set about exonerating Haber, anyhow. But it keeps eating on Jimmy. He feels that it falls to him to square things for Dad."

"He's built that way," Lex agreed. "And I certainly can't blame him for it."

"I'd like to see justice, myself," Amy said, with rising feeling. "But where is there any justice in this country?"

"None now. Later, maybe. *Quién sabe?*"

Amy shook her head doubtfully. "Lex, I don't see how you can ever beat Palgrave at the polls, the way Big John hopes. Palgrave controls the election machinery all over the county. Even if our side won, who would ever know it? The votes wouldn't be reported honestly."

"If our side loses again," Lex said, "Big John figures to demand a recount by disinterested state officials." He sighed. At the moment his mind was weary of campaign problems. He said, "Don't you worry about supper. Jimmy and I'll eat down town, and I'll have them send something up for you and John."

"Why thank you, Lex. I guess I am tired."

Something showed in Amy's eyes that he guessed was appreciation. It dawned on him that few cow-country women got much consideration along that line.

He headed back downtown. He was still short of the main street when he saw Haber and Palgrave coming into town, in sight for only seconds as they crossed the intersection ahead. Lex pulled up his shoulders. To his knowledge, it was the first time Palgrave had ever let himself be seen openly with Hap Haber.

When Lex reached the main street, he saw the pair swing down in front of the distant courthouse. At that moment Doc Cornell came out of the barber shop, his face fresh shaven and glowing. Seeing Lex, he nodded with a quick smile, simultaneously biting the tip from a cigar.

Cornell had twenty years of frontier medicine behind him. He had an intimate acquaintance with more families than any other man in the county. Big John had induced him to buck Palgrave for the county judgeship because of the high regard in which Cornell was held in the nester colony and even on Slick Ear, as well as throughout the cattle sections. Though he was the key figure in the fight, the opposition's main hope of wresting control from the machine, he refused to campaign openly, preferring to stand on his reputation.

Now Cornell made the inevitable note of Lex's bruised face and said, "Jenkins told me about your squabble with Haber when I got my rig, this morning. I thought you were running things on a higher level than that, boy." But the man's gray eyes twinkled.

"Haber got a taste of his own medicine," Lex said, "and I mean a taste." Cornell visited Big John at off hours so that it had been a long while since Lex had talked with him. So Lex added, "Any change in Big John?"

Cornell nodded thoughtfully. "As those things go, he's doing well. I'm considerably cheered at the way he took the shock of that explosion. But no man ever had more self-control than John. I doubt he even batted an eye when the roof blew off his house."

"He sure cussed his head off, though," Lex remembered. "But stayed put in bed like you said he had to. What's his chances of ever getting well again?"

"It's like I told you at the start. Anything can happen."

"This election's getting rough," Lex said. "Pretty soon there won't be any of the peace and quiet he needs if he's going to stay with us. There's already been things happen I'm scared to tell him — and it's the same way with Holly. What are we going to do when it gets worse — stick cotton in his ears and lock his bedroom door? Palgrave tried to kill him last night,

Doc. John thought so from the start. He might try again, and how can an invalid fight that way?"

"John started it, you know," Cornell said, grinning dryly. "And if it kills him, let me tell you something. It's the happiest way he could die."

"I reckon you're right, Doc," Lex said, and was considerably relieved as he watched Cornell go on down the walk.

Then his attention swung on up the street. A courthouse underling had hurried along the far sidewalk and entered the door of the *Daily News*. Presently he emerged with Frank Renwick, who flung Lex a quick, masked stare. Lex waited there until he saw the pair disappear into the courthouse. A chill ran through him. He thought, *It's about the gun ruckus. They're holding a powwow.* Renwick's being called into it meant that there was need of the *Daily News*.

When he returned to the *Call* office, Lex found that Sara had taken paper and pencil and gone forth to make her rounds. He sat down at his desk, an idea turning in his mind, inspired by what he had just seen. The *Call* had as much a part in this campaign as the *News*. The weekly was not due to come out for days yet, but he was considering the effect of bringing out an extra at once, given over to an account of the rustling on Toadstool and what it had brought forth. He could tell the whole story. An honest rendition of the happening might cause Palgrave to drop any idea he had of making something out of the death of Lefty Farnol.

Lex picked up a pencil, reached for a block of paper and began to write. He composed objectively and with the greatest facility he had ever known. The words flowed to the paper without conscious effort, a factual account of what Toadstool had experienced, of what the machine had tried to make of it, of its effort to follow through with blackmail. There was no need to underscore, interpret or in any way weight what had been done and said. What he did not say would speak eloquently to every man in the country.

When he had finished writing, Lex went to the old type cases. He had employed a tramp printer for a time, at the start, and from him had learned the rudiments of the business, the typesetting and operation of the old hand press. He began to set up the story then, with the same smoldering drive in which he had written it.

The door opened quietly, and he turned to see that Sara had come in. She looked at him, puzzled. "You're getting an early start this week, aren't you?" she asked.

"We're coming out early. Tomorrow morning, if we can cut it. Where's Jimmy?"

"He was here for a while this morning, then he left. He won't hang around here when I'm alone. He's down on me, and I don't know why."

Lex grinned at her. "The devil you don't — it was him seeing us with our minds on something besides business. Seems to be rooting for somebody else."

"And she's awfully nice." Sara carried a bag which she put down on a work table. "I've got some news but not nearly enough to fill up the paper yet. Want me to write you some jokes?"

"Never mind. We'll come out thin, hoping nobody'd be of a mind to hunt for the second page after reading the first."

"That's easy. I won't tone up your language, and everybody'll spend the day trying to figure out page one. What's the big story?"

"Rustling on Toadstool, which Conbuck might want to parlay into a trip to the hangnoose for me. There's the copy, if you want to read it."

"Lex — not really!" Sara picked up the finger-smudged pages and was still while she read. Looking up finally, she said, "So that's what happened. It relieves my curiosity but, believe me, not my anxiety. Those people have the knack of making things come out the way they want."

"That's why I'm printing the thing. I'd rather be the one breaking it than trying to defend myself against Renwick's account."

"Do you realize that you're going all out? Palgrave might be forced to ram it through just to refute you."

"Or he may feel inclined to call it a smear and not stir up any more stink."

Sara looked thoughtful, saying, "Can I help?"

"Sandpaper that language you were talking about. If we can get the front page made up tonight, we'll run off a lean issue in the morning."

She went to the little table she used for a desk, carrying the copy he had not yet set up. Sunlight, cooled and filtered by the front window, spilled upon her slender figure and seemed to set her hair on fire. It drew his mind away from the job. He had never seen anything as strikingly alluring, not even Amy, and that interest was getting too completely out of hand.

He was not aware that twilight was coming in until Sara lighted a couple of lamps and set them where they would help him. He had most of the main story set up by then and was trying to figure out the composition of the rest of the issue.

Then he thought of something and gasped, "Good God, Sara — run over to the Gem and have them send a couple of meals up to the house. I told Amy I'd do it, and I plumb forgot."

"You bet. How about you?"

"I'll chew my mustache."

She slipped out and was back very soon.

"Quitting time for you," Lex said.

"I feel like I'd ought to help you."

"There isn't much you can do. The big sweat will come in the morning. You might get here bright and early, if you can pry yourself out of bed."

"That's easy. The nicest part of my day is starting off to work each morning. This is the only place I'm ever happy, any more."

Softly he said, "Come here, Sara. We'd better get together on that."

She moved around the table, the yellow lamplight bringing out the lustre of her eyes. She looked up at him, lips parted. "Here I am," she said.

He turned from the forms, forgetting completely what he had intended to make clear to her first, and caught and drew her into his arms. Again she had shown him her answer to his prying question about her wants, the one she had refused to answer in words. She came against him strongly, swiftly — then just as quickly she changed her mind and twisted away before he had found her lips.

He said, "Sara . . ." then heard the crash and turned to stare in dismay at the floor. He had not locked the form, which her movement had knocked from the end of the work table. It was the big one, carrying the nearly completed rustling story. It had hit on edge, and the type was scattered hopelessly across the floor. The work of hours was ruined.

"Oh, look what I did," she moaned. She stared at the floor, then at him, with remorse twisting her face.

He grinned but had to force it. "I reckon it can be done over."

"Let it go until morning. You're worn out. I'll be here before sun-up to help."

He nodded vaguely. Anger seeped up from somewhere, and it was not because of her carelessness alone. She had introduced the matter of their private and increasingly exciting relationship herself — and at what struck him now as a curious time. Until then he had forgotten the skinning knife that had got out of his office so curiously. He was as yet less suspicious than deflated and annoyed, with a sense that somehow she had made a fool of him.

Contritely, she said, "If I could set type, I'd do it over tonight, myself."

"Never mind. But you'd better go home before we put the press out of business, too." He knew he sounded sharp. She lifted her head, staring, then turned toward the door.

When she had gone out dejectedly, he rolled a cigarette. He had thought of something else and was beginning to wonder more deeply. She had come into his arms from one direction, swept out in the other, skidding the form along with her. Maybe she hadn't been as carried away as he had assumed. Somehow that skinning knife had got into Haber's hands, and he had tried until now to keep from digging into that question.

A quick opening and shutting of the door drew his attention. It was Jimmy who came in. Lex grinned and nodded. When he saw the tenseness of the boy's face he stared.

"What's the trouble, Jimmy?"

The boy came on into the full light of the lamps, Lex watching with rising concern. There had been the dread of bad news from the house ever since Big John took sick.

"Lex," Jimmy said, "I've got to tell you something that you won't like. There's monkey business going on at Abel Jerome's. There's something fishy, too. I know how you feel, but that don't change it. Sara and Abel are in cahoots with Hap Haber in some kind of deal."

"Kid, you're imagining things," Lex said sharply. But what Jimmy said was so completely in line with his own disrupted thoughts that he did not sound convincing.

"Am I?"

Lex let his weight sag back against the table, and his jaw slacked. "Cut the deck a little deeper, then — I don't know what you're driving at."

"I see things," Jimmy answered. "Mainly because I been watching Haber like a hawk. I've known for a long while that he goes to the Jerome house — too damned often, if you ask me."

"Trying to shine up to Sara," Lex snapped, surprised at his intensity. "She told me about that, and she didn't seem to like it."

Jimmy's jaw was stubborn. "Haber goes there when Sara ain't home, too. And it's more than him having his eye on a girl."

Lex managed to grin. "Amy told me how you feel it was Haber who shot your dad. And I think he's prejudiced you against the Jeromes."

Jimmy's voice had a mature rasp that was shocking. "It sure was Haber who killed my dad."

"I know. Amy told me why you think so, and I reckon you're right. But don't let it work on your imagination. Jerome's a veterinary. He takes care of nester and plateau livestock, as well as the cattle outfits. He's the same as Doc Cornell — he's got to go where he's needed and see whoever comes to his place. Where have you been all day?"

"That's just it," Jimmy said, and his spine had stiffened. "I spent most of it laying on the rim above Jerome's house. One of Conbuck's deputies drove in there with a buckboard. Mighty jumpy and cautious about it, I noticed. They run the buckboard into the barn, and when it come out it was loaded with a tarp covering whatever it was. The deputy got aboard and drove off."

Jimmy tossed his head. "From where I was, I seen the cuss hit the road to the nester colony. Add it up, Lex. A Conbuck deputy gets something that's been hidden in Jerome's barn and he takes it out to the nester flats. Is Jerome doing all the veterinary work through the sheriff's office? It happens there's a tack room in Jerome's barn he keeps locked tight. I got a chance to sneak in there once when nobody was home. I seen that locked door."

"He has to be gone a lot," Lex said stubbornly, unable to get Jimmy to see how horribly he was being swayed along the boy's line of thought. "Likely there's things he wouldn't want stolen. It's no crime to use a lock, kid. I got one on that door. Now, you hustle home and set Amy's mind at ease about you. Then come back to the Gem and eat your supper. Amy was too played out to cook."

Jimmy sighed, then turned and went out. For a long time afterward Lex stood motionless. He was weighing Abel Jerome, realizing that the man was even more of a mystery to him than Sara. A gray-haired, granite-featured man, he was as big and rangy as the Starlight sons. He had a withdrawn, almost truculent manner and was highly proficient in his profession. He was kept busy and could hardly be pressed for money, with his daughter working as well. Jimmy was imagining things, but Lex wished he didn't sense something beyond analysis, or perhaps beyond facing, within himself.

CHAPTER
NINE

Lex felt an ache in his shoulders that came from long stooping, and he stared with dull eyes at the type scattered across the floor. A big part of the night would be required to repair the damage, and he realized now how much the past hours had taken out of him. He thought of his own delayed supper and wondered if hunger had something to do with his deep and restless irritation. He got his hat.

He entered the Gem to find Jimmy finishing his late meal. Lex took a counter seat beside him. But the boy was sullen, seeming to feel that he was getting no co-operation and little recognition. Lex did not try to jolly him out of it, knowing that it might work the wrong way. When he had finished eating, Jimmy, his shoulders held high, paid for his supper. Lex had meant to do it, but this small pride in Jimmy marked the change that became more and more evident. The kid was growing; it was a hard time in any life. Jimmy went out of the place without waiting for Lex to walk home with him.

Coming out of the restaurant, Lex felt fatigue press him all the harder. He flung a look at the *Call* doorway, down the street from him, then abruptly he swung off in the other direction. Full night was on by the time he reached home so that he could not see what progress had been made with the repair work. But he got a shock when he entered the house. Amy was seated in the living room, her knitting on her lap. Across and in his old leather armchair sat Big John, grinning like an imp.

"Dog my cats, John!" Lex gasped. "After all this time, you've taken to cheating on Doc!"

John chuckled. "Cheating, hell. He says I can exercise my saddle muscles a little from here on. I showed that sawbones I'm a tougher turkey than he took into account."

"But you've been up longer than he allowed," Amy said severely. "I couldn't get him back to bed until he'd thrown a surprise into you, Lex." But her eyes said that she had not tried very hard.

"Come on, John," Lex said. "Back to your soogans. Want me to tote you again?"

"Stay away from me, man!" John bawled, and he brought up a fist. He would have used it if Lex had persisted.

When he had helped his father hobble back to bed, Lex said, "You've got some fine friends, John. I should have made a list of all the men I saw working around here, today. Some of them would have surprised you."

"Amy told me who they were. How did you find things at the ranch?"

"Coming right along."

"I doubt that. Holly's taken to dodging me. He's hiding something."

"He gets a lecture and a hatful of free advice every time he shows up here, John. I don't blame him."

"Next thing I know," John said, "he'll be telling me hands off — the way you did."

"I hope he does. You've made him responsible for Toadstool, so give him the authority."

"It ain't so much Toadstool."

"What then? Your fear he'll turn into another George Galtry?"

"I guess maybe that's got me scareder than I ought to be," John admitted. "But I can't help it." He pulled the covers over his ears which was his dismissal, the sign that he wanted to sleep.

Lex got Jimmy, lighted a lantern and they put up a couple of cots in the old carriage house. Jimmy remained to turn in but Lex started back to the main house. The moon was up, and he could see the new shingles on the roof, the outlines of the restored kitchen flue. Somehow that evidence of spontaneous generosity, of enduring friendship, was the most hopeful evidence he had seen so far in the campaign.

When he climbed the front steps, he saw that Amy had come onto the big, vine-covered porch for a breath of fresh air before going to bed. She rose as he came up, and he spoke quickly.

"Don't go yet."

"It's late, and we're both worn out."

"Too tired to sleep, myself."

She stopped before him, looking up into his face in sudden intentness, and he wondered what it was that she sought to find there. Then softly she said, "I want to thank you for last night."

"What did I do except pack you out of that room? And in a state of dress that would scandalize the town if it knew?"

Her laugh was even softer than her voice. "Much more. It's the first time I was ever called a lovely girl."

"Dang my hide, you were faking."

She shook her head. "Groggy and not sure that I wasn't dreaming it. Until I sounded you out last night and you were so embarrassed."

"I ought to tan your skirt. No, I ought to do a better job of the other thing I did. You know that I kissed you?"

She looked away. "I guess I was pretty groggy."

But she didn't move when he stepped toward her. He put his hands on her arms, and she looked up at him with the starlight glinting in her eyes. Then she whirled away, as Sara had done, and he did not understand because she had been the one facing the sidewalk.

Holly's voice said from behind him, "Don't mind me, folks. That makes a real pretty picture."

Lex swung about. Holly had turned in from the street walk. He came on to the bottom of the steps, where he halted. His voice had carried its old, bantering lightness, while moonlight revealed a mockery on his face that was not an habitual characteristic. The stretch of private walk was too long for him to have got that close without Amy's being aware of it. Holly guessed as much, and this was what had changed him.

Lex said, "Kind of late. What brought you to town?"

"Something I figured to have out with John."

"He's asleep."

"Then I'll wake him up."

"Wait, Holly — I reckon I know what it's about. You and Pitt have decided to tie into the Slick Ear bunch. But your conscience got to bothering you, so you decided to tell John first. Doc let him set up for the first time, today. He'd steam up plenty if he knew you meant to take the law into your own hands. Don't do it."

"Hell with you."

"I mean don't tell John."

"I think he's right, Holly," Amy said then.

Her quiet remonstrance did what Lex had despaired of doing. Holly shrugged but relaxed and remained where he stood. He said, "All right, then. But I'm tired of feeling like a sneak, doing one thing and pretending to him I'm doing another."

Lex said, "Well, I don't know that you're being smart making a play against Slick Ear. But I won't try to talk you and Pitt out of doing what you think you've got to. I'll tell John you come here beforehand to tell him, and I advised against it. He can take something that's already done easier than he can accept something coming that he don't like."

"Then I'll get going," Holly said. "I got a lot to do." He nodded and moved off down the walk to the street.

For a long moment Lex looked at Amy. He said, "Mean to tell me that you couldn't see him coming?"

"I was looking at you. What's the difference — or are you just ashamed of yourself?"

"I — well, I guess I got a little of John's worry about Holly. He's dead gone on you, Amy, even if you don't believe it or even don't want him to be. I — well, I reckon you know I am, too. Holly and me kind of talked it over at the ranch, today. I got to admit I've been holding back for fear of what it would do to him if I was lucky and cut him out."

"I tried to make him understand," Amy said readily, "that he's immature in his emotions. He's got to grow up sometime, hasn't he?"

"Amy, I've got to tell you. There's a wild streak in the family I didn't know about till lately when John told me. We had an uncle who went bad and hit the owl hoot. I'm not trying to take advantage of Holly telling you that. It could break out in me just as easy. Something's been coming to a head inside of me for a long time. John could be doing his worrying about the wrong one."

"I like a man with spirit."

"If it's got a bridle on it."

"That's right. Good night."

"Amy, which one of us is it?"

"What makes you so sure it's either one?"

She was gone through the doorway, and after a long moment he retraced his steps to the carriage house.

He awakened the next morning with instant excitement, remembering that he meant to bring out an extra edition of the *Call*. As he thought it over in the gray light of dawn, the consequences of failure rose before him, awful in their enormity. He swung out of bed and began to dress, his jaw set. He was going to publish that rustling story for the whole county to read, and the hell with whether it backfired.

He had his breakfast at the Gem. Sara had her own office key, and he had expected her to be there early, as she had promised, but when he reached the printing shop she had not arrived. He opened up, neglecting the sweeping and tidying he usually attended to the first thing each morning. He set himself at once to making up the printing form again.

He had been at it only a short while when somebody came through the door. He looked up to see not Sara but her father, Abel Jerome. He rarely encountered the man and now, staring at him, he had that odd dual sense-image that tells a man he has experienced something before in the limbo of lost recollections.

Jerome's rangy body was a little stooped, but his face was strong, impatient. He said curtly, "Sara won't be here, this morning. She's not feeling very good."

Lex looked steadily at the man, remembering the suspicions Jimmy had voiced the night before. As if resenting the inspection, Jerome swung and walked out. Lex frowned, but mainly out of an immediate worry. Sara's unexpected default left him short of help he had counted on. He could go home and get Jimmy to come down, but Sara was trained in the work and the boy wasn't. There was nothing to do but try to get the issue out alone.

It was around ten o'clock when one of the *Daily News'* delivery boys appeared in the open doorway to call, "Take a look, Mister Starlight. You're on our front page — that is, your ranch is." The lad threw a paper into the room and swung off. He was grinning.

Lex went to the paper, picked it up and unrolled it. His eyes widened, and his jaw muscles began to pull tight. There was nothing extraordinary in the make-up of the front page. But the right-hand column had an arresting headline:

POLITICAL PLOT FOILED

Lex read on, apprehension jarring through him. It was a full account of the rustling as Haber, Conbuck and Palgrave had put it together yesterday in the breaks. The slanting, the clever emphasis lent it by the skill of Frank Renwick made it a horrible, damning thing. Fascinated, he read on, then — halfway down the column — he came to a small box superimposed:

NESTER LEADER MURDERED

Tom Lerner was shot down in his doorway during the night by a mysterious assailant, Sheriff Conbuck informed the *News* this morning. He suspects a tie-in with the political situation and promises a vigorous prosecution of the case. Lerner had grown dangerous to political upstarts, says County Judge Palgrave . . .

He could read no more because of the sickness churning in his stomach. It was too much to grasp: the

Call's scoop on the story that had been wrecked by Sara's carelessness — or Sara's design; the shock of Tom Lerner's death by murder; the new and completely sinister aspect lent the situation by that murder.

He remembered the courthouse conference yesterday, into which Frank Renwick had been called so hurriedly. He recalled Sara's initial uneasiness on learning that the *Call* meant to print an extra. Had she set him back to give her time to warn Renwick, who must have gone to press in the night? *You might as well face it*, he told himself — but he could not bring himself to put the whole of it in words.

He went to his desk and sat down, still holding the *Daily News*. Renwick had given his stories a beguiling validity, seeming entirely reportorial on first reading but disclosing a careful editorial slant on closer inspection. Lex knew that few in the county would give it that careful a scrutiny. A charge was stronger medicine, in frontier journalism, than the most cogent of refutations, and Renwick had seized upon that fact.

Lex thought he understood the reason for this quick, heavy follow-up to the trap that had been sprung in the breaks. Palgrave, with Conbuck's party, had left the scene and headed back for the nester flats. They must have seen Lerner again to learn that he had slipped completely out of their clutches. So Lerner had been condemned to death, swift and merciless. He was the one man who would have made it possible to establish the truth, and the one candidate who might have carried the nester colony for the opposition ticket.

"We're whipped," Lex said aloud. "And you might as well admit that, too."

But he would not admit it, any more than Big John would have. Something was beginning to stand out in his mind. There had been no mention of the death of Lefty Farnol in the fight in the breaks. Palgrave did not want to build a murder charge around the death of an outlaw that most people had despised. But the voters would care about Tom Lerner, not only the nesters but most of the cowmen, because he had been a respected man and an influence for peace between the two factions.

Doc Cornell came in then, his face a graven image. He closed the door behind him, although the morning was growing hot. He carried a copy of the *News*.

His first thought sprang from his responsibility as a man of medicine. Tersely, he said, "We've got to keep this from John. The gall of them printing those quotations from Haber and Lerner to make Toadstool look dirty as hell. Now Tom's dead and can never deny that he said exactly what they printed. Lex, one of you Starlight boys is going to be charged with that murder."

"I reckon. Doc, how can a man fight the devil, himself?"

"I dunno. But I know lies can be fought with truth."

"I was about to print that story myself, and print it straight. Renwick caught on somehow and beat me. Now my story would only look like a puny defense."

"Print it anyhow. And I want you to quote me, the way Renwick quoted Palgrave. Say Doc Cornell declares the whole thing to be a frame-up, based on the murder of an upright and innocent man. Say that if it keeps up, he intends to ask the state to take over the county government until an honest election can be held and trustworthy officials installed."

"You'd do that?" Lex gasped.

"And get results. I've always tried to keep out of politics. But we've got an honest governor, and we happen to be pretty good friends. Palgrave knows that. Print what I said for its effect on him more than on the public in general. He could railroad anybody he wants, Lex, given a reasonable basis in fact to work with."

"I know, and I'll do it."

"Meanwhile, watch your step like you've never had to watch it before."

Jimmy arrived just as the doctor left, and Lex went back to work. It was noon when they had got the old press started on its grumbling way. Jimmy helped, and by two o'clock they had the town delivery of the paper ready for him to take out. The boy went at once, alone, while Lex set to work getting the country papers ready to go out on the stage and the mail routes. The printing and folding kept him busy for hours. Jimmy did not come back to the shop, but Lex was not alarmed. They wouldn't try more rough stuff on a kid with the situation grown so delicate.

CHAPTER
TEN

With his work done at last, Lex washed his smudged face and hands. The letup caused him to think again of Sara and her part in this thing. The first shock was wearing off, but a sick bitterness remained. He examined that again, still without finding a convincing reason for her, at least, to join forces with the political machine. She was not lazy nor covetous nor ambitious for easy gains. It was hard for him to accept that she had not been sincere in her frequent bitter outbursts against the work and rottenness of the Palgrave gang — and particularly against Hap Haber, with whom Jimmy had linked her and Abel Jerome.

Somewhere in his heart, Lex found a lingering loyalty to Sara. There was more, much more to the situation than he had yet learned or even begun to divine. He wished he could talk with her frankly but doubted the wisdom of that just yet . . . Then his thoughts were broken off abruptly by a development on the street.

A cavalcade of riders had started past the *Call* office windows, pulling him to the front door. A half-dozen men rode along in double-file, known outlaws from Slick Ear Plateau. Two of them had been in the gun battle in the breaks. Another was called Two-Gun Tull, while the three men remaining were his helpers in the running of a greasy-sack cow outfit on the plateau. They were open friends of Hap Haber, men who were believed to constitute a gang under Haber's leadership.

They rode dispiritedly, and Lex noted their empty holsters. But his attention was mainly on the three Toadstool riders who came along behind. They were Pitt and Holly and a puncher named Slim Mahan. They had guns in their hands, and their faces showed a determination to use them if necessary.

Passing Lex, Holly said quietly, "Come up to the courthouse. We got some buttons, even if we failed to catch the snake that rattles 'em."

"Haber?"

"The slippery son just wasn't where we could corral him."

Lex swung back through the door and got his hat. The Toadstool riders did not know of the latest development, which would take the edge off their present triumph. He went out onto the street, joining a growing crowd of curious people moving toward the courthouse. When the horseback party reached that structure it pulled down in front. A horseshoe-shaped gallery quickly formed in the dusty street and across the sidewalk, causing the Slick Ear men to look cowed and jumpy.

Pitt Berts looked at a man on the walk and said, "Go in and tell Conbuck to get off his lazy backside. If somebody else must do his job, he can at least run the jail right. We've got some customers here."

The man swallowed, then swung up the wide steps.

Half the town's population seemed to be on hand by the time Conbuck appeared in the courthouse's double front doors. His cheeks were tight with shock, with disbelief.

"What's this?" he demanded.

"They're wanted men, Conbuck," Pitt returned. "A richer haul than you ever made, and we're giving them to you free of charge. Us boys dropped over for a talk with Two-Gun Tull this morning, only he hadn't invited us. We caught all these jiggers there. You could clean your slate of some unsolved crimes if you sweated them a little."

"This is an outrage, Conbuck!" Tull yelled. "Since when can honest citizens be arrested this way?"

"What's this got to do with honest citizens?" Pitt asked. "But since he mentions it, Conbuck, I better explain that we made what's called a citizen's arrest."

"You got to catch somebody breaking the law before you can do that," Conbuck snapped.

"We did, Conbuck. They were passing around a jug of corn whisky without any revenue stamp. There's a lot of moonshining in the Slick Ear country, even if you have winked at it. You going to lock them up?"

"Why should I?"

Pitt grinned for the first time. "One reason is that you might be embarrassed if you up and turn them loose. We figured you wouldn't look over your dodgers the way an honest sheriff would. That's why we're late getting here. We sent a man in ahead of us to wire the U. S. marshal the description of this catch. You're going

109

to get hold orders on the lot. So you better have the men here to back up that wire."

"You — you wired the marshal?" Conbuck gasped.

"And I bet the man's on his way here, already."

Lex was beginning to feel the first satisfaction in days. Pitt did not know it yet, but what he and Holly had done fitted in perfectly with Doc Cornell's published threat to call for state intercession in the local situation. Conbuck must have seen the *Call*'s extra edition, for he looked sick. Western settlements were touchy in their independence and quick to resent outside interference. But Conbuck saw before him aroused, resentful men who realized that might be the only way relief could be obtained from the long-entrenched machine.

He said, "All right. Take 'em around back. I'll lock 'em up. But don't ever think you're getting away with this."

The Toadstool men left town immediately, aware that their presence created an explosive situation. Lex talked with them only a minute. "It was Pitt's idea," Holly reported. "And he's the one who went in there and got 'em, me and Slim only covering him. He's either going to make a first-rate sheriff or a corpse."

"I take it you haven't seen the extra the *News* got out," Lex said. "The caper yesterday is all written up — their way. Worse than that, somebody killed Tom Lerner on his own doorstep, last night. There's no question in my mind that he turned on Palgrave completely and signed his own death warrant. One thing's sure. I'd rather be accused of killing Lefty Farnol than Tom. I got a hunch one of us is going to be charged, and Doc thinks so, too."

"Good God," Holly said and swallowed.

"But maybe what you boys pulled will help us," Lex resumed. "I printed our side of the story, and a statement of Doc's that he's thinking of asking for state intercession. You've sent for the marshal, who's sure as hell going to rob Hap Haber of his best men. And he'll ask Conbuck some questions as to why it had to be done by plain citizens with a supposedly efficient sheriff around."

"It could slow Palgrave," Holly reflected. "Or it could hurry him up. When a man gets desperate, he gets reckless along with it. If he had Tom Lerner murdered, he's got a hang-noose over his own head."

Lex had barely returned to the *Call* office when there were running steps on the walk beyond the door. He looked up to see Amy hurry past a window and, his heart racing, he met her at the door. Her hair was coming loose, and she panted as if she had run all the way from home.

She gasped, "Where's Jimmy, Lex? I told him to come home the minute he'd delivered his papers! He should have been back an hour ago!"

He stared for he had forgotten the boy completely. He said, "Why, I thought that was where he is."

"He's not — and suddenly I got scared, Lex! I don't know why! But something's happened to him — I know it has!"

"Now, take it easy," he said gently. "He's been playing detective a lot lately. That's what he's up to now." But her fear had leaped to him, going all through, and he doubted that he had kept from showing it.

"We've got to find him, Lex."

"Sure," he agreed. "But you go home. I'll go over his route, and I'll take a look at a place where I know he's been doing some spying." He placed a finger under her chin, adding gently, "He's all right, Amy."

"He's not, and I'm afraid — terribly."

Somebody's heels hit the sidewalk again at that moment. Another figure passed the window. Then Dude Carmen, Conbuck's chief deputy, stood in the doorway. A dapper man, he stared at Amy with openly disrespectful eyes. Then he flicked a cool glance to Lex.

"Conbuck wants to see you, Starlight," he said.

"And figures I should do the walking instead of him?"

"That's right."

"What's on his mind?"

"A murder," Carmen said. "A man named Lerner was killed last night. Shot in the face standing in his own doorway in his underwear."

"Is this an arrest?"

"Not yet. Conbuck just wants to see you."

"No!" Amy said. "Lex, you've got to find Jimmy!"

"Something happen to Jimmy?" Carmen asked her and looked owlish. "That's too bad because Starlight won't have time to look for him. He's got to come with me or I'll have to come with a warrant. That would be bad and a lot more final than Conbuck wants to make it if he can avoid it."

"So he's leaving the door open again," Lex said. "I'll get a choice between throwing in the sponge and being locked up. You go back, Dude, and tell the man to go to hell."

"You're making a mistake, buck."

It was Amy who gave Lex the break, throwing herself at Carmen. The deputy hadn't expected it and swung her way, throwing out his hands. Lex hit him, clean and hard, on the underslope of the jaw. Carmen's knees broke, and his head flew back and he went down under that one hard punch. Lex fell to his knees, clapping a hand over the fellow's mouth before he could make an outcry. Amy flung herself on his threshing legs.

Drawing Carmen's gun, Lex used its barrel to rap the deputy hard across the head. Carmen went slack. Rising then, Lex was aware that he had done a perilous thing. He was making himself a fugitive at a point where he needed all the freedom possible. But he had acted to help Amy and not out of his own forethought. He helped her to her feet.

"I hit the man," Lex breathed, "because he was insulting to a lady. Remember that, Amy. He stated flatly that he wasn't arresting me. You remember that?"

"Yes. But he'll get a warrant. Lex, what will you do?"

"They'll have to serve a warrant before it's any good," he said. "And to do that, they've got to catch me."

"But Jimmy?"

"I promise you that I'll find him."

He drew Carmen to the door, took a look along the street, then rolled the man out onto the sidewalk. He closed the door and locked it. He said, "Slip out the back, Amy, and go home. Don't tell John a thing. Don't let him see that you're scared."

"All right. Will you come there?"

"Soon as I can. I've got to have time to think. It looks like I'm on the dodge, already."

She left, going through the back way into the alley. A man came along the sidewalk, saw the inert Carmen and paused. He flung a puzzled look through the window, then went on, shaking his head.

Lex strapped on his shell-belt, checked his gun and pulled on his hat, his face grim and wooden. He also left the shop by way of the back door, stepping into the alley and following it until he came to the rear of Doc Cornell's combined dwelling and office. He moved to the door and rapped cautiously. In a moment the doctor appeared there to stare at the gun on his hip.

"What's happened now?" he asked sharply.

"They've made their jump. Conbuck sent Carmen to bring me in. I knocked him cold, and I'm on the dodge, I reckon. But I had to see you."

"Come in," Cornell said, and he stepped back.

Lex explained the latest developments, concluding, "I can't think yet. I've got to locate Jimmy. Then I've got to steer clear of the so-called law till I've found a way to beat this thing. You keep an eye on John and Amy, will you?"

"Don't worry about them, son. It's you that's got me scared. But you're smart. It won't do to let them clap you into jail. Lex, maybe I'd better turn to the state, now, the way I threatened."

"Not for my sake," Lex said. "It'd break John's heart if his own sons got so helpless they had to yell for help. Don't do it, Doc."

"Luck, then — and I'm afraid you'll need it."

Lex paused in the alley, a moment later, uncertain as to his next move. It would take time for Carmen to get back to the sheriff's office unless somebody carried him there. It would take even longer for Conbuck to get a bench warrant issued. For a short while, Lex felt, he could move about in safety.

He went to the livery to get his horse, entering the stable by the rear door. He came upon Jenkins in the gloomy interior, and the man stared at him in hard surprise.

"You on the prowl or the dodge, coming in that way?"

"I'm hunting Jimmy. You seen him?"

"Not since he left the paper. That was quite a while ago. The news today sure makes a man dizzy. One paper says one thing, the other just the opposite."

"Which did you believe, Trink?"

"Well, it's like this. It's getting right unhealthy for a man to think at all."

"Some time between now and election, man, you and a lot of others have got to make up your minds."

"Mine's made up. But I can vote in secret, and I'm scared to have even a fence post hear me talking." Jenkins looked about warily, then added, "Lex, there's something I been meaning to show you about your saddle. Step into the harness room a minute."

Lex followed the man into a dark, dusty room. There Jenkins went on in a voice that was barely a whisper.

"But I've got to risk some talking, Lex, because I like you as well as being on your side. I'm scared to death. I been told that your horse was out of here last night, and that if I think or say otherwise I'm apt to get a bellyful of lead I never swallowed."

"Conbuck?"

"Did I say who? All I know is, I'm supposed to say, if asked, that you come in and got your horse around midnight, last night. And that you never brought it back until just before daylight, at which time the horse showed a lot of hard riding. And one other little thing. That you tried to slip me a twenty-dollar gold piece."

"Thanks, Trink. They'll have to do better than that, though, if they get me hung for killing Tom Lerner. Help me saddle my horse, will you? I don't have much time."

He rode out of the stable by the side door and turned down that same street. Gaining the one that led to the river bridge, he crossed over. This part of town was quiet, empty, lazing in the heat of the day. He kept going, his mind stilled suddenly by a sense of dread. Then he thought, *Why don't you face it? You're going to Jerome's. If Jimmy got into trouble, it'd most likely be there, him prowling around the way he has . . .*

The place stood at a short distance beyond the last town houses since Jerome's work required corrals and a barn. But it was a neat establishment, shaded by old trees and set against the long, high cliff. The yard about the house was green and well kept. He knew that Sara

116

liked to work there. When he swung down at the gate his pulse skipped, for she was seated on a bench built around the trunk of one of the trees and had seen and was smiling at him. Trailing reins, he stepped through the gate and walked toward her.

She rose from her place and came toward him, wearing a fresh dress of green gingham that transformed her into a personality that he had never before seen. He had thought of her only as she appeared at the shop, groomed and gowned for the public eye. But this was the girl who kept house, who devoted her time and thoughts to a woman's affairs. It softened the aura about her, and for all his worries he thought, *Why, right now she's got the look I like in Amy.*

She said, "Hello," as they met on the path. "Did you come to fire me for letting you down like I did? I just didn't feel like working." She seemed tired and more than a little uncertain. Then she laughed. "And why the horse? I walk it four times a day."

He made her meet his eyes and held them closely while he said, "Have you seen anything of Jimmy? He hasn't come back from delivering the papers."

"Why, I did," she said readily. "Jimmy and young Andy Keck. They were riding Andy's old plug, and they had fishing poles."

Lex let out a long sigh of relief. "I'll take the hide off of him. Going fishing when Amy told him to check in with her as soon as he got the *Call* delivered. Which way were they heading?"

"Up the river, and it wasn't too long ago."

"Well, he's all right, anyhow." Lex started to turn, his mind relieved and free now to report that fact to Amy then take whatever his next step must be. But he doubted that Conbuck would be beating the brush for him very soon. From what Trink Jenkins had told him, he knew the sheriff had hoped to bluff him into some kind of deal through the threat of blackmail. With a United States marshal due to arrive soon, he would not be anxious to be actually holding such a prisoner. He began to lose his first panicky impetuosity.

He said, "Did you hear how the *News* beat us with an extra?"

She looked rueful. "It was all my fault, too. You'd ought to blister me again."

"I'd like to know how Renwick got wise to my plans. He must have been for he brought his paper out hours earlier than usual. Something sure tipped him off."

She looked up at him closely then, murmuring, "Lex, you're laying those shots in a little close. Are you trying to imply that I might know how he caught on? I'd say that both you and Renwick recognized a good idea and jumped on it. He just happened to beat you." She lifted a hand to her mouth suddenly, her eyes stricken. "Ah — that type. You're wondering if I knocked it off the bench on purpose."

"You didn't think my extra was a good idea at the start, Sara," he reminded her. "I'm sorry. But there's some other things make it necessary for me to ask some unpleasant questions. At first you kind of tried to talk me out of it, didn't you?"

118

"All I thought of at first was the danger. Then I began to see how important it was for you to be the first one out with the story. I tried to help, and you don't know how badly I felt about spoiling all that work for you. I woke up this morning with a sick headache from it, so bad I just couldn't get out of bed till noon."

"You look all right now."

"I feel fine now. But by the time I did, you'd got the paper out. Lex, it shocks me how much you distrust me. I never even suspected it."

Her misery touched him, but too many things crowded for him to quit until he had satisfied his mind. He said, "Haber comes here right along, and you've told me so. But Conbuck's men do, too — and your father has made no intimates like that at all on our side."

"So it's him you really distrust."

"I reckon so. What does he keep locked in his tack room?"

She straightened at that and drew in a long, slow breath. "I don't know what you mean. But if you'll come with me, I'll let you take a look for yourself." She turned without his answer and went across the yard toward the looming old barn.

He was halfway ashamed of himself as he followed, but he knew that nobody would be happier than he if she could give herself a clean bill of health. She seemed confident. The big door of the barn was shut but not locked. She waited for him to shove it open on its iron track, then slipped ahead of him into the dim and musty interior.

119

It was no different from any other barn, he saw. There was a wide center aisle and at its end an old hack stood under a cover of dust and cobwebs. Openwork on the right side gave onto stalls for horses. There was a haymow above and a pile of hay beneath the laddered opening to the mow. Along the left ran a feed bin, the locked tack room and then an open storage space with nothing in it. Lex saw little reason for Jimmy to have grown so suspicious about the place.

Sara picked up a rock that had chocked a wheel of the hack. She said, "Dad's got the key, but if you'll whack the lock a couple of times, it'll open. Go ahead." He saw from her eyes that she was more than willing — she was eager to have him do it.

"Never mind. I'm sorry, Sara."

She let the rock drop and watched him closely. "What did you think might be in there?"

"Nothing. But somebody else did. Never mind."

She smiled at last, relieved and suddenly buoyantly happy. "That makes us even!" she breathed. "I'm a blunderbuss, and you're a nitwit!"

The smell of cured hay was heavy in his nostrils. In that moment the vision of her laughing up at him stilled his thoughts and released his feelings. He stepped toward her, and she lifted her arms, readily. Hunger poured out of him and it came back to him from her, unabashed now, open and intimate. She hesitated a second as he swept an arm under her knees and lifted her up, and as he fell to his knees with her in the nearby hay, she moaned, "Oh, Lex . . . Lex . . ." Then she was done with doubts.

120

CHAPTER
ELEVEN

He was first aware of a start in Sara's body. She pulled away from him, sighing, and then he heard the jar of a slow horse coming into the yard. He stared down at her, and she whispered, "We're caught. It's probably Dad." Rising, she slipped to the opening in the door and went on out.

Lex followed, feeling guilty, his head still filled with its sweet memories of her. But he was not of a mind to conceal his presence. Abel Jerome sat his saddle, looking steadily at Lex as he came out of the barn. Sara said nothing, and Lex could think of nothing to say, himself.

"I see you're feeling better, Sara," Jerome said dryly. She smiled. "A lot."

She said nothing to explain why she had taken her visitor to the barn. Lex still found himself tongue-tied. Jerome looked at one and then the other, then swung down from his horse. He led the animal over to the gate of the corral. There was no reading his thoughts. But a prickling in Lex's spine told him what a dangerous man that one could be. There was a lot more to Abel Jerome than he wanted anybody to see.

Sara followed Lex to where his own horse stood at the front gate. There, in a low voice, she said, "I don't want him to know that you were suspicious of him, Lex. I'd rather he kept on thinking what he wants."

"It's your say."

"Oh, darling — I love you so. Believe that, no matter what comes — believe it no matter what."

The intensity of her voice caused him to pull up his shoulders and stare, and it was like looking at her for the very first time. The thing in the barn had been a new one with her, and she had left him with no doubt as to that. Even then he had begun to suspect that it came out of a very deep feeling in her, that it was not what he had wanted it to be — a mutual dalliance. Her intensity now lifted in him a profound regret, making him remember the caution he had meant to exercise, his cooler knowledge, back there, that they could not meet this way on a common ground. It was too late now; the thing was done.

Rising to the saddle, he smiled, said, "*Hasta la vista*," and rode out . . .

It was well past dark when he reached Toadstool. He thundered into the ranchyard, and though it was familiar territory it gave him a sense of shock to find it so quiet. Holly's tense voice called, "That you, Lex?" and he sat his saddle in stunned surprise. Armed men came out of the shadows all about and moved warily toward him.

"It's me!" he reported. "What in hell's up?"

Holly's shape emerged from the group. Lex swung from the saddle and walked toward him.

"Nothing yet, thank God," Holly answered. "But there will be, and I'm glad you come out. Tom Lerner's wife sent their kid over here this evening. She wanted us to know that some hotheaded nesters have got hold of new guns and ammunition aplenty. They're talking about taking it up for what they think we done to Tom."

"New guns?" Lex gasped.

An actual physical distress filled him. Guns were not occupational tools of the nesters as they were with stockmen who had always to keep on the lookout for predators. If the flat's hotheads had been arming themselves, it was strange that the town hardware man had not tipped somebody off.

As if reading his thoughts, Holly said, "Renegade guns, and likely the work of Hap Haber."

"Renegade guns?" Lex was still parrotlike in his shock. That locked tack room again, the covered hack Jimmy had seen pull out of Jerome's barn, driven by a Conbuck deputy, to head for Kinsey Flats. Jimmy had been right about that. At the same time Sara was exonerated, for her complete willingness to open the room could have come only from ignorance of what might be found in there.

"That's what the Lerner boy said," Holly was continuing. "His mother's brother — that Louie Andrea — is one of the soreheads. Around fifty nesters have been armed and given a hundred rounds apiece. The inquest was held over there today, then the funeral. Afterward the squatters made their plans. But the Lerner woman wanted us tipped off — which proves that Tom must have swung back to our side before he was murdered. And she must know it was the machine that murdered Tom."

"Why in hell would Palgrave want to start up a range war?"

"Lex," Holly said tiredly, "we don't know that Palgrave's back of everything that's going on. He's brought together a lot of greedy men without any scruples whatever. You get a bunch like that, and there's always the ambitious ones in it. Somebody even honing for power and the top place. We don't know who all we're up against, and that's scared the hell outta me ever since the Lerner boy come over."

Lex nodded, for the first time taking a good look at that possibility. Hap Haber was entirely capable of acting on his own hook, even at the expense of double-crossing his vaunted friends. Lex remembered also that Frank Renwick was restless and dissatisfied in the position of an obedient underling to Palgrave. There was also Abel Jerome who, Lex was now convinced, tied into it somewhere.

"You're right," he said. "The election might actually be only a sideshow. Maybe just a cover for something bigger. I never thought of that, and it's sure time we did. I'm on the dodge, boys. Conbuck sent Dude Carmen to bring me in for a so-called talk. Carmen threatened to get a warrant if I didn't come along voluntarily. I batted the man one and hit leather. We've got to make big medicine and make it now."

"Brother!" breathed Pitt Berts.

"I've got the pot," Holly said, "if somebody can come across with the medicine."

124

"Right off," Lex said, "I'm going over and have a talk with Tom Lerner's woman."

"But why?" Holly gasped. "Louie Andrea lives there. He'd drop you in your tracks."

"Mebbe. But I've got to find out what all she learned about Tom's frame of mind after we seen him last in the breaks, and what went on between him and Palgrave's bunch. If she had the courage to warn us about the nesters, she's got enough to speak her piece to that U.S. marshal you boys sent for."

"We never sent for him," Pitt rejoined. "But it's likely that he'll come, when he gets our wire. We can't wait for that."

"I'm going to talk to her."

"Better all of us go, then," Pitt said.

Lex shook his head. "Less chance of trouble if there's only one of us. It's plain she can't handle the other nesters or she'd have had no need to send us word. But it's likely she can keep Andrea from going hog-wild. And I'd better get along."

The others protested again, but he ignored it and rode out, taking a fresh horse from the Toadstool night band. A full moon had come out, lighting the range and bathing it with a look of deep peace. He kept shaking his head as he rode. This country had never been meant for the violence that men had brought to it. But violence lay deep in men's minds and its curse would always be upon the world. It had been so from the beginning.

He had to pass through the breaks on his way to Kinsey Flat and, as he entered, he found them lonely but untroubled. He passed the place where the short, vicious fight with the outlaws had taken place. He soon reached Pilot Rock, where the trail split to strike off for the plateau or for the nester flats directly south. The country was so chopped up that he came within sight of two waiting riders before he or his horse was aware of them, and before he could even react a voice bawled at him.

"That you, Hank? How's it look over there?"

He did not recognize the speaker, but instinct reported that he had run spang into a tight situation. It was too late to conceal himself and all that was left was to take a bold tack.

He called, "Not good — and you'd better hit for home like I aim to!"

"Hey — who are you?"

He was pretty certain from their high-peaked hats that they were Slick Ear outlaws and would have been less puzzled to come upon nesters gathering here for the jump-off at Toadstool. As the man yelled his second inquiry, Lex spurred his horse, sending it rushing along the south branch of the trail. There were long, exposed seconds in which he feared they would start shooting. But they had not yet come out of their bewilderment.

Grateful for the fresh horse under him, he bent low, urging the mount onward with gentle insistence. He heard rearward hoofs strike the hard earth and drum up a running beat. His horse easily kept its distance, yet the pursuit persisted, and since he did not know what he might come upon in the nester colony itself, he began to doubt his ability to carry out his purpose and even to escape being cornered.

Some lightning instinct showed him his chance at the end of another mile. Ahead loomed the rim and the break that let down onto the wheeling, open flat. But a stock trail ran along the rim through chophills that would screen a rider. Without conscious decision, he came to a halt, swung down and whipped the riderless horse on along the bench trail. Running, he pressed himself into a rock crop, dropping flat. The rushing pursuers came driving on, pulling in at the rim. They could see no horse breaking onto the flat below, and their sudden quietness let them hear the animal that still pounded through the choppies on top the bench. Lex grinned coolly when they took the bait and swung after it.

Then he was alone with the question of whether to head back for Toadstool or to go on into the flat afoot. He hoped it would be some time before they caught his horse and discovered the trick. When they did, they would think it more natural of him to head back the way he had come. Tom Lerner's claim was on this edge of the flat. Lex decided to go on with his business.

But he moved north along the rim top for a distance, wanting to get directly in back of the Lerner claim before striking out into the open. His high-heeled boots made the going uncomfortable, and on this course there was no broken path to follow. When he had put a little wild country behind him, he stopped to smoke a cigarette and rest.

Stars blazed above him, reaching from the rough, high horizon north to the ruled line below. From his point of vantage the flat was a gray-black obscurity, infrequently broken by a pinpoint of light declaring a human habitat.

The heat of the chase and the wildness of his environs had raised in him a rare elation, and on its heels came a rush of thoughts put aside in recent hours. Without premeditation, he had entered into a new relationship with Sara. Somehow his initial regret, with the confirmation of how much he had meant to her, was losing a little of its force. He had taken more than he had thought was still hers to give, and she would always stand apart from the women he had possessed in easy give and take. It surprised him to learn that a man could not take a good woman without forever feeling for her a special tenderness.

Yet this was not the reason for his diminished regret. He was beginning to wonder if he might not find in her the other qualities he instinctively sought in his mate. The bold, new run of his thoughts forced him to consider Amy and the regard in which he had held her for so long. He was neither fool nor idealist enough to relinquish claim to her because of a brother's similar interest. But he was puzzled as to why he could never turn upon her the rushing male insistence, the *must, must, must* that had brought about the thing in the barn. The problem was too great for him and, rising, he began to look for a place to drop down to the flat.

He was not too familiar with the nester settlement but knew how to reach Lerner's place from his visits there when inducing the man to run for public office. It lay out from him, presently, wholly dark and eloquent in the danger it might hold for him because of the man Andrea and the boiling hate now upon the flat against the Starlight family. He feared also that there would be dogs to betray his approach, but none declared itself.

He came quietly upon the house. The days of the tar-paper shacks were over, and Tom Lerner had built for his family an ample and attractive farmhouse. When his arrival brought no alarming reaction, Lex went boldly to the front door and knocked.

A long moment passed before a voice called through to him, and the tightness left his chest at its feminine timbre.

"Who is it?"

"Lex Starlight, Missus Lerner. I've got to talk to you."

The door opened at once, with a woman in a nightgown dimly seen in the space disclosed. He had grown casually acquainted with Rita Lerner on his visits with her husband, and had developed both liking and respect for her.

"You shouldn't be here!" she breathed. "Louie's asleep upstairs, and he's apt to give you trouble!"

"We must talk."

"Not here."

"Where, then?"

She was silent a moment, then said quietly, "Go into the orchard. I'll be there in a minute."

Nodding, he slipped quietly away. A hip-roofed barn loomed behind the house, while off to the right ran a family fruit orchard. Moving in among the trees, he waited. Presently she appeared, bundled in a coat.

"What is it?" she said uneasily.

"I wanted to thank you for warning Toadstool," he answered, "but more than that brought me. Those smuggled guns — it looks like somebody's trying to start another war like the nesters and stockmen fought in the old days."

"I know," she moaned. "But what can we do?"

"You've proved you don't believe we killed Tom because he'd turned on us. And you must have suspicions as to who really did."

"Yes," she admitted. "But that's all. I didn't see it happen. Somebody came in the night, just like you but on a horse. Nothing was said. Tom opened the door, then I heard a shot. The horse went away on the run. By the time I got to the porch, Tom was all in a heap. The horse had swung around the orchard, here, and I didn't even see it."

"You told that at the inquest?"

"Yes."

"They've got a man in town," he explained, "who's supposed to build onto that. He's been ordered to put me on a horse at just that time. It catches me on a mean spot, and I've got to play tag till the thing's shook down. But here's what I come to ask you. You may not have heard that our boys rounded up Haber's gang today and made Conbuck lock 'em up. They wired the U. S. marshal, and there's a long chance the man will be here within a day or two. I wondered if there was anything you could tell him that would throw light on how Tom really come to die or about who smuggled guns in to the nesters."

130

"I don't know what went on between Tom and Palgrave," she said, "after they came back from the breaks. But I know Tom was furious, afterward, feeling that Palgrave had tried to make a fool of him. He was all the more determined to help break up the political machine."

"That would help a little," Lex said. "What do you know about the guns and ammunition?"

"One of Conbuck's deputies brought them here."

A cold feeling riffled up Lex's back. He had guessed, he had all but known, but now Abel Jerome's part in the plot was a certainty.

He said, "If the marshal comes, and I arrange for you to see him secretly, will you try to help him get to the bottom of things?"

"Yes."

"Thanks, ma'am. I'll get in touch."

"Where did you leave your horse?"

He laughed. "Had to part company with it when I bumped into some Slick Ear citizens in the *mal país*. I reckon I'll have to hoof it home."

"We've got horses in the barn, if you don't mind riding a plug."

"It might lead to trouble for you, ma'am."

He left at once, relieved that no added trouble had come from her sleeping brother. Louie Andrea, he recalled, was one of the hotheads planning revenge upon Toadstool, and the fact that he was sleeping seemed to rule out this night as the time set for it. So what had the Slick Ear riders been doing in the breaks, and what had been the meaning of that inquiry, "How's it look over there?"

CHAPTER
TWELVE

It dawned on him, as he trudged out onto the flat, that the night's ride had put him equally distant to the ranch and to town. By cutting an angle toward the town, he would come to the little cow outfit Johnny Dalton ran on Daisy Creek. There he could get the loan of a horse and cut the walk ahead of him in half. He decided on that course and changed direction, aware also that he would have to cross the country into which he had sent his pursuers on a wild goose chase.

Coming to the rim, he prowled its underslope until he found a place where he could get on top. A few minutes walking, and he cut the stock trail that had served him that night to good advantage. He turned south on it, the way he had sent his horse, but without hope that he might be able to pick the animal up. An hour had passed since then. In that time they must have caught the horse, discerned its brand and swept off in an effort to intercept its erstwhile rider between there and Toadstool.

Thus it was that, half an hour later, he was dumbfounded to come upon a little hill-locked meadow and discern the saddled animal at a halt, grazing serenely. Then it dawned upon him that this was the place where they had found the horse. In their rush, they had not wanted to be impeded and had left it here. It was something no man could have counted on, and he was grateful for the stroke of luck.

He started over the meadow boldly. The horse swung its head to look at him. Its reins were still over its neck, and he feared that it would bolt and run. But it went on feeding and let him come up on it. Grinning, he caught the reins and reached for a stirrup. He was half up to the saddle-seat when a voice bawled out from somewhere.

"Bat your ears with your elbows, cowboy, and set right still!"

Two men rose up from a ground swell on past the horse's position.

Feeling a flutter in his stomach, Lex raised his arms. They came on aggressively. Closing the gap, one said, "By damn, it's Lex Starlight himself! I told you that, whatever Toadstool rider it was, he might be worth waiting for!" They both held guns in their hands.

"You boys are real cute," Lex drawled. "And now what happens?" He had identified them, a couple more Haber men who had not been caught at Tull's place by Pitt and Holly.

"Just want to know what the hell you're doing in these parts this time of night."

He had to offer something and did not want to involve Rita Lerner. He said, "Seen a man messing around on the basin side. Must have been that Hank you mistook me for. I thought I was tailing him when I bumped into you, but he seems to have given me the slip."

"Well, we outguessed you," the lead man said. "You figured we'd read your brand and try to cut off your backtrail. Then you'd try to pick up your horse and save your heels."

"All right," Lex said boldly. "Now you know who it was. Good night, gents."

"Just a minute, buck. You're coming with us."

"Where?"

"To town. I know a man there who wants to talk to you."

"Conbuck?"

"Yeah. He don't realize it yet, but I think he'll want to know why you pay visits to the nester flats during the night."

Lex repressed a sigh. He had not fooled them as to his destination and was all the more determined that Rita Lerner should not become involved. As he saw it now, she was the most important witness he would have if he was to be charged with murdering Tom Lerner. Palgrave must realize that, and the woman stood in danger that this night's contact had increased considerably.

He said, "All right, let's go. Where's your horses?"

"Yonder across the meadow. Ride ahead, Starlight. You'll have a gun on your back." The man came forward and took his gun.

Lex rode indolently to the brush on the downmost side of the little meadow. The two horses were hidden there, and his captors rose quickly to leather. One swung ahead then, and the other fell behind. The leader pointed their way on along the stock trail, a little later letting down to the flat and crossing over to the nesters' road to town.

Nowhere in those few miles did Lex see an opportunity to try to make a break for it. His gaze slid constantly about him for he had no intention of falling into the hands of his enemies if he saw a fighting chance to avoid it.

He saw no such opportunity until the road came into the river bank, not two miles from town. Cottonwood and alder skirted the stream, sometimes in a thick belt. He took care not to look at the timber and let another half mile fall behind. Then, momentarily closing off his breath in his tension, he drove his spurs hard into the horse's flesh, swung it sharply right, bending flat as it crashed among the trees.

A gun spat savagely, both men yelling as the forward rider cut about, then he heard their horses enter the brush behind him. The river at this point was not easily crossed, and that fact was his hope of escape. Limbs slapped and scraped him, and once he was nearly knocked out of the saddle. He knew he was shut from sight of the pursuit, because nobody tried to shoot just then. He came to the river-bank and spurred his horse down the sharp slope to the water.

Excited, the animal gave him trouble before he got it to enter the water. When it reached swimming depth, he slid from the saddle, letting himself be towed beside it. Guns began to crackle behind, lead pocking the water about him. Then he was up on the other side, exposed to the shooting until he had gained that brush. He didn't try to mount but ran, dragging on the reins of the willing animal, and then the concealing brush surrounded them.

He rose instantly to the saddle. Dangerous as it was, he had to enter the town, reach the Starlight house and obtain a gun. His pursuers showed no taste for entering the water and crossing as he had. The ford was about a mile on downstream. He broke out into the clear and again sent his horse rushing forward . . .

He left the horse in a gully at the edge of town and followed the depression on in. He moved on from the start of the buildings with increased caution, sticking to alleys and back streets until he was in behind the Starlight house. He neared it to grow surprised at the lamplight showing in the downstairs window for by then he knew that it must be close to midnight. Crossing the back porch quietly, he found the door locked and rapped. He was still so wet that water dripped from his clothes.

When he heard cautious steps in the kitchen, he called, "It's Lex."

The door opened hurriedly, and he saw Amy's shape. Her voice, although at the level of a whisper, carried a terrible urgency.

"So you couldn't find him, either."

For the first time in hours he thought of Jimmy, gasping, "Good God, Amy — isn't he home yet? He went fishing up the river with Andy after he'd delivered the paper."

136

"He couldn't have — Lex, where did you hear that? When it got dark without him coming home and no word from you, I checked with Andy. He hasn't been fishing. He hasn't seen Jimmy since this morning."

He could only stand and stare down at her stricken eyes. Sara had lied to him about having seen Jimmy — there was no other explanation. It had been smooth, at the drop of a hat — or she had expected somebody to inquire about him and had prepared that story.

"Who told you that?" Amy insisted in a torn voice.

"Sara. Amy, Jimmy's been spying on Abel Jerome. Since then I've learned it was for good cause. If anything's happened to him, Jerome's responsible. I'm going over there, but I've got to get Big John's six-gun."

He didn't tell her how dangerous it would be to do that with Haber's riders in town already, reporting on him to Conbuck. But he had to do it — he didn't even consider an alternative. He slipped into his father's bedroom to find him asleep, got John's .45 and thrust it into his empty holster. Amy was distraught enough that she had not asked a question about him, and he was glad of that. He patted her reassuringly on the shoulder and went out.

He dared not risk the river bridge crossing to Jerome's part of town, so he made his way downstream until he reached a place where he could wade across. He climbed the far bank with sloshing boots again. Most of the houses along the street ahead, which he was obliged to walk boldly, were darkened for the night. As he neared the Jerome place, he detected lamplight. He had no time to investigate the premises before making his presence known. Crossing the porch openly, he laid his knuckles on the door.

He had to rap harder before anybody came to answer him. It was Sara. She opened the door, fully dressed, to give him a stare as stricken as the one he had just seen on Amy's face. It convinced him that he was on the right track. His face a set rebuke to her, he stepped in without invitation.

Seeming to get hold of herself a little, she forced a smile. "What on earth brings you here at this hour of the night?"

"Curiosity as to why you lied to me about Jimmy. Amy's seen Andy, and Jimmy hasn't been with him all day."

"Why — I thought it was Andy . . ."

"Don't lie to me any more, Sara. I've had more than I want of that, already. If you have any idea of where Jimmy is, you'd better tell me."

"But I don't know, if it wasn't him and Andy I saw. Lex — what's got you to acting like this?"

"Your father's helped run guns to the nesters. I know that for sure. And I know why you were so willing to open that tack room for me. The guns had gone on, and there was nothing in there for me to see. I know the why of the rest that happened. Women have tried to foul trail that way for a long, long time."

"Lex — don't say that — don't . . ."

"You know something about Jimmy and, by God, you'll tell me now."

"You'd better come talk to my father," Sara said in a spent voice.

He followed her out of the entry hall into a room deeply shadowed in the light of a single, shaded lamp. Then he spotted Abel Jerome, who was seated in a chair beyond the lamp and watching intently. Seeing him for the first time without a hat, his face sharply lighted as he bent forward, Lex had that bewildering thought: *I've seen him somewhere — before he ever come here to live . . .*

Aware of the close attention, Jerome frowned and pulled back from the brighter light. He said, "I heard the conversation — without understanding all of it. What's this about Jimmy Kemble?"

"You helped Palgrave arm the nester colony, Jerome," Lex said flatly. "I know that for a fact — and Jimmy knew it before I did. He fell into your hands, somehow. What have you done with him?"

Jerome chuckled suddenly, saying, "Maybe I see light. Sara explained why she took you to the barn. So it's guns you thought was in that locked tack room."

"What then?"

"Stock tonic. It's my own preparation and expensive to make. I keep it locked up. If you want, I'll take you out and show you."

"Conbuck got a deputy that sells the stuff for you?"

"What do you mean by that?"

"Jimmy seen a deputy drive a buckboard into your barn and come out with it loaded. The rig headed for Kinsey Flat. With stock tonic, of course, for some sick settlers."

"Jimmy never saw that happen in my barn that I know of . . ." Jerome stiffened, and his glance slid to Sara.

Through the next seconds, something held them all arrested. Lex quickly discerned that it was a thumping sound, off some place but still inside the house. Lex's hand stabbed down, and when it came up it held the .45 with its barrel lined on Jerome.

"Neither one of you move. I'm going to have a look at the next room."

"It's a limb!" Sara cried. "There's one that brushes against the house."

"There's no wind tonight."

His smile was bitter, like a struck blow. He backed through the archway and across the hall toward a shut door on the far side. Jerome nearly rose from his seat, then settled back. The door knob turned under the hand behind Lex's back. Swinging then he saw a bed with a trussed figure lying upon it.

He said, "Jimmy!" in relief, for the boy was able to twist desperately in his bonds.

"Go ahead and cut him loose," Jerome said. "We won't give you any trouble."

"I trust you two like sidewinders. Sara, come and get him out of that."

She did so, moving on weighted feet. Jimmy had been there a long while for he had trouble getting up. He had been gagged as well but, Lex realized, had managed to twist about so that he could thump his bare heels on the wall.

Jerome had not left his chair when the three of them went back out.

"What kind of a pat excuse have you got for it?" Lex asked.

Jerome shook his head. "Not pat — but an excuse. You won't believe it, but I saved that boy's life by taking him a prisoner and holding him here. I can't tell you more than that — not yet."

Lex laughed. "When? After you've collected your price for all this dirty work?"

"You have no idea how wrong you are, man — no idea."

"How did it happen, kid?" Lex asked Jimmy.

Jimmy was working his stiffened arms, and fury had gathered in his face. "They took me prisoner, all right — and Sara helped. She called me into the house when I come by with the papers. Before I knew it, her dad had hold of me. They tied me up and gagged me, and I've been in that bedroom ever since."

"Dad," Sara said brokenly, "I can't stand this."

Abel Jerome looked at her in what seemed to be genuine sympathy but he slowly shook his head. Then, himself sounding a little desperate, he said, "Lex, for Jimmy's sake, you've got to understand that he's marked. We couldn't tell you, him or anybody else without getting it ourselves. You've got to believe that for his protection, no matter what you prefer to think about us. He's fooled around too much for his own good."

"I heard what he told you, Lex," Jimmy cut in. "I sure did see a Conbuck man drive a buckboard outta his barn with a load of something hid under a tarp."

A certain dignity had returned to Sara. Quietly she said, "You don't have to believe anything, Lex, except that Jimmy's in mortal danger. Now that you know, take him somewhere where he'll be safe."

"Don't worry about that," Lex returned. "Go on, Jimmy. You're long overdue home."

There was no time to settle the thing. He had Jimmy, and every minute he loitered about getting the boy home increased the danger to both of them — for he was willing to accept that Jimmy was in grave peril from the sinister machine.

When they were well away from Jerome's place, Lex said, "If they were actually trying to save your life, Jimmy, it would be from Hap Haber, wouldn't it?"

"If they were."

"You figured he was the one you saw leave our place after the explosion. Maybe he saw you."

"When it comes to Haber," Jimmy said, "there'd be an even better reason for him to kill me. I know he's the one who shot my dad, and I told him so that day on the bridge."

"Ah," Lex said on a long breath. "Jimmy — Jerome could have been telling the truth."

"Well, they told me they were doing it for my own good," Jimmy admitted. "But that was all they'd say. How'd they know Haber's intentions, Lex, if they haven't been in on the inside business all along?"

142

"I reckon you're right," Lex said, and his last lingering hope of finding excuse for Sara died in his heart.

They had crossed the river below the bridge, again, and were up in the business part of town but following along a dark back street. Lex was marking that fact when suddenly Jimmy gasped.

"Lex — look out . . ."

It was too late and proof that his luck had run out. Two men had turned the corner ahead and were staring his way. Lex shoved Jimmy behind him and plucked his gun as one of them yelled. He knew by then that they were part of Sheriff Conbuck's big crew.

Quietly, Lex said, "Cut across lots, Jimmy, and get home as fast as you can. I'll be there pretty soon if I can make it, but I might have to cut straight out of town. Go on now." He had to give the boy a shove to get him started.

CHAPTER
THIRTEEN

When he swung his attention to the corner again, Lex saw that the Conbuck henchmen had ducked back out of sight. It dawned on him that, at the moment, they might care less about him than about Jimmy and could be moving to head the boy off. Lex cut out after the boy, not able to see him now but confident that Jimmy knew how to cut a bee-line to the Starlight house.

Gun in hand, he followed in long strides. There was no discounting the fact that the whole town was alerted against him, which meant that there was a good chance that the house itself was being watched. But he gave no thought to his own chances of escaping. He could not until he knew the kid was going to be all right.

He came cross-lots to the place and, pausing for a second, could see no sign that it was being kept under observation. Rounding the rear corner, he climbed to the porch and knocked gently so as not to alarm those inside. It was Jimmy who threw the door open, Amy coming behind him, her face brilliant in its relief and her gratitude.

He said, "Doc Cornell was going to take you under his wing. Has he been around?"

Amy nodded. "He was here for a while. But somebody came for him and he had to go. That was just after dark."

"Who came for him?" Lex asked, frowning.

"Some nester. He said his wife was sick."

An all-gone feeling formed in Lex's chest. Doc and no one here beside himself had known of the warning Rita Lerner had sent to Toadstool of the nester uproar over her husband's death. That animosity would be directed toward everyone on the opposition ticket, as well. But Doc, even had he known, would not have let fear keep him from answering a call. He simply had not been put together in that way.

Nonetheless, fear blew its cold wind through Lex's mind. Things were shaping swiftly for a showdown, and Cornell was a greater threat to Palgrave than Tom Lerner had been. Tom had died in a vicious act of treachery and, the way things stood, there was more than one nester on the flats who could be induced to decoy Doc into the same kind of trap.

Or, and the alternative was even more awful, somebody could have observed that Cornell was here with Amy and Big John, and that ruse could have been developed to get him away from the house. Lex was not dismissing the possibility that the thing had been perfectly legitimate, but he dared take no chances. He had to warn Big John, which meant telling him things it might be better for him not to know.

He found that his father had been kept awake by the continuing excitement downstairs. Lex looked down at him, the tired face faintly discernible in the moonlight seeping into the bedroom.

He said, "John, this thing just isn't going to be settled at the polls the way you hope."

"And why not?"

"Too much has happened. Maybe Palgrave's afraid to trust a vote, now. Maybe there's a lot more than just another election involved. I'm not even sure he's the only one trying to push through a dirty plan. Listen, now. I've got to tell you things we figured you'd best not hear."

"Shoot," John said promptly.

Lex told him, omitting nothing at all. When he had finished, Big John was silent for several minutes.

"Help me to my chair in the living room," he said finally. "Then fetch me my gun. You get back to Toadstool and help the boys. Nobody's coming into this house without my permission."

Lex did what John wanted, saying finally, "I reckon I need your six-gun, John. One of Haber's hardcases has got mine. But there's your rifle. Jimmy knows how to use it, too."

"Don't you worry about us. Just you be on your way."

Lex stepped out the back door, but Amy followed and stopped him on the porch. She said, "I'm so grateful to you, Lex. Now you take care of yourself." Rising on her toes, she kissed him.

She would have slipped back, but he caught her arms above the elbows and searched her face. The feel of her flesh was pleasant but less than the exciting thing that had swept him into heedlessness the day before. He knew in that moment that he loved Amy deeply and always would. But it was not necessarily the feeling that lay between prospective mates.

A faint twist of bitterness changed the set of his face. Until now he had found himself swayed between two women. And now, when a man faced it, he had neither one.

He found his horse waiting undisturbed at the place where he had left it. A full moon still hung over the range as he entered it on his headlong ride for Toadstool, and he knew that daylight could not be far off. The wheeling sweeps had once held for him a solitude that he liked. Tonight they spoke only of the elemental basis of all being, all life. What could a man know, especially about himself, and what could he trust?

Far off in the pre-dawn darkness, something jarred him out of his thoughts. He was on Starlight land now, cutting an angle across country toward the headquarters site. He rode on for a distance without understanding what had dug into his consciousness. Then he realized that what seemed a placid tick-tick sound was really a crackling in the far distance. It was gunfire, in the direction of headquarters, and a charge of energy shot through him.

He spurred his horse to a sloping rush. The steady punching of angry guns soon was unmistakable across the night. The ranch was under attack. But he was calm suddenly, settled. No right-thinking person in all the county had wanted this kind of thing, but it had been forced on the basin in some kind of awful and unseen stubbornness. He was ready for the fight. If that made him wild, then he was shaped in the image of George Galtry perhaps more than Holly was.

He rode the last few hundred yards with care, dropping into a draw that concealed and let him come in close. The sound of the crashing guns was sharp and furious when he halted and swung down. Leaving the horse, he prowled onward, emerging onto the flat where the ranch structures stood.

The building shapes were softened in the fading moonlight, but he could detect the flash of many guns. They were like fireflies, he thought, cutting through the sooty gray. He halted, breathing in a shallow way. He tried to pick up the pattern of the fight, uncertain as yet as to where he belonged.

Without knowing which side they represented, he fixed in his mind the location of several contesting guns. Somebody was shooting from the big hay barn, at the maw of the loft. The gun's flash angled downward at a target on the ground. Lex decided that this fighter was a Toadstool man, thoughtfully stationed in the haymow before the onslaught came. Then, somewhere in the ranchyard, a man let out a sudden, stricken cry. The sound of it quivered in his shoulders. Elsewhere a gun blazed out and its sound was echoed all along the reach of the yard.

Slugs tore into the walls of the buildings, thrown by steadily barking pistols and heavier punching rifles and carbines. He moved in closer, picking out cover between himself and the yard and making bent runs.

148

He reached a clump of brush that stood against the horse-pasture fence. He nearly fell over a man.

Fortunately the fellow recognized him at once, saying, "That you, Lex? I figured it had to be one of our boys coming from that direction."

It was Curly Wilson. Lex said, "You all right?"

"Took a slug across the ribs, but it's not bad. We got 'em good when they barreled in. They figured to catch us asleep. We sure scrambled their eggs, and now they're pinned down so they can't get away. It must have given Hap Haber a turn."

"Haber?" Lex echoed.

"I heard his name called in the confusion when it backfired."

For the first time Lex understood the meaning of the riders he had tangled with near Pilot Rock. The man Hank he had been mistaken for had been sent in to scout the situation, and the pair in the breaks had been waiting for him.

"So he took command of the nesters."

"I ain't sure they're nesters," Curly said. "These jiggers fight too good. I think it's a Slick Ear bunch getting even for us taking in that bunch of Tull's. We've got a scrap. It must have been two hours ago they hit."

"I hope it isn't nesters," Lex said.

He crawled to his right, flattening when a gun cracked close ahead and a bullet whined above him. The gun blasted again and yet again. He parted the dry grass and took a look at a forward obscurity. Somebody was in beside the roofed porch of the house and had picked him up. The shots were probing. He brought his

149

gun up, waiting for a fiery blob to bloom in his sights. He caught the target and pulled the trigger. A yell of pain followed the shot.

He kept going along the fence and presently crawled under it. He could see the front of the hay barn from the new position and most of the other structures in the yard. But every man shooting in this confined area endangered himself unless he changed position constantly.

That stricture had mixed the men badly, confusing the targets. A slug shrilled above him, a stray bullet. His glance ranged the yard uneasily. Haber's outlaws were trying to slip out of the trapped confinement of the area next to the house. Day was near, and they had no taste for being pinned down there with light helping the other side.

Anger ran through Lex, a violent and choking feeling. Haber couldn't get away with this and make the further use of it he always seemed to make of his triumphs. Lex flung a hasty, reckless shot at a gunflash against the house. In the next second he paid a price. Somebody used the flame of his gun to lay in a shot. It hit Lex's ear stingingly as it whipped past.

He dropped flat, his belligerence under control again. He felt his ticked ear and brought down bloody fingers. Flattening out, he waited for developments. He saw a man crawling in the shadow of the blacksmith shop. Not sure who it was, he had to hold fire. Then the man in the loft opened up and the one by the smithy wall quit crawling.

Somebody yelled violently. It was the voice of Haber, unmistakable, and he yelled, "Bust outta it, boys! We've run out of time!"

Guns opened all along the side of the house and out at the corner of the woodshed. It steadied Toadstool, rather than otherwise, for this swift obedience to Haber's order separated friend and foe. The would-be raiders came out in a loose line, weaving and shooting their way.

Lex got to his knees and fired a couple of quick shots. They were crowding too close. He slithered for the fence again, rolled under the bottom pole and got into the brush. He had bought himself a moment to reload his gun. Afterward he sat there quietly and picked off a man who tried to gain the same cover.

But it had become clear that Haber was only trying to drive out of entrapment. From what Lex had observed, they must have left their horses opposite the side he had ridden in on. His lips pinched grimly. He was determined that they should not get away until they had paid in full measure for this attack.

He crawled back to where he had left Curly Wilson, who had moved over against the fence to lay in a helping shot where he could, wounded but without a drop of fight drained out of him.

"Where you going?" Curly asked.

"Aim to see if I can run off their horses."

Curly grunted something more, but Lex moved on. His ear hurt, but that only goaded his anger. Presently he rose up, cut over the fence and made a bolting run along the peaceful side of the ranchhouse. He found that the outlaws had left their horses on the far side of a poplar windbreak built along the windward side of headquarters. He waited, concealed by the trees. There were horseholders, as he had feared.

And men were already pulling out of the fight, bolting for the windbreak and escape. Realizing that he still could do some good, Lex stopped one. Others came on and, dropping to a knee, he cut loose at them.

He saw a man stumble forward and fall. The others scattered but kept running. He shot again, and by that time they had figured out where he was. Guns blazed at him, although the runners kept going. His gun went empty, and before he had reloaded they had gone to horse and were away, the guards fleeing with them. The fight was over.

The ranch's survivors were calling to each other across the yard. Lex went in. Reaching the edge of the central compound, he yelled, "Holly!" and heard Pitt's gruff reply.

"He's out on the range, Lex. We got to thinking they might hit at the herd instead of headquarters."

Men moved from their separate little forts as Lex walked on into the yard. If there was life left in any of the several raiders lying about the place, it no longer carried fight. Half-a-dozen Toadstool men walked or dragged themselves into the open. Lex came up to Pitt, who had been the one in the haymow and who now stood outside the barn's lower door.

Pitt stared at his men as they disclosed themselves in the yard, which was brightening now with dawn.

He said in a tired voice, "It looks like we're short four men. Holly took five with him and left nine of us here."

That tally hit Lex hard. There weren't that many men left on their feet.

A puncher who had been scouting around came up. He said, "There ain't a hit nester in the bunch, and I don't think in the ones that got away. It was all Slick Ear work — that or the nesters scared out when they realized it wasn't going to be a lead-pipe cinch."

"I don't think they had any part," Lex said. "I seen Rita Lerner. Louie Andrea was there asleep. If he'd had any inkling of this caper, he'd have been getting set for it. Boys, I'm glad it was this way. Had there been nesters mixed in, this would have been the opening battle of a long and nasty war."

His nicked ear had clotted and was no longer bleeding, but it had smeared the side of his neck with blood. He gave no thought to that as they made a grim reckoning of the cost. Jack Andrews lay dead at the corner of the barn. Curly Wilson and two others were wounded. Yet it would have been far worse if Toadstool had not been forewarned.

The inspection disclosed that Haber must have brought a dozen men against the ranch and had left half of them behind. It was a testimonial to Toadstool shooting that not a one of these was still alive. Lex's only regret as to that was that an even greater toll had not been exacted. They were men the country would be far better off without, members of a class the Palgrave machine had been letting drift in for so many years.

"Slick Ear or nesters!" Pitt growled at last. "This thing won't stop short of hell! We lost Jack Andrews, and him as fine a man as ever forked a hull. You won't get our boys to call it a day till Haber's down with lead poison, himself."

"I grant you that," Lex agreed.

"And you and me had better run a chore, Lex. I'm uneasy about Holly and his boys."

"Too far for them to hear what went on here," Lex said.

"Too far for us to hear what went on out there, too," Pitt retorted. "I'm going to have a look. I can see why the nesters might hit us like this out of spite. But why would Haber? There wasn't a thing for him to gain here. There was — out on the range."

"The herd?" Lex said sharply. "Pitt, maybe you're right. Haber might simply have pinned us down here while another Slick Ear outfit hit the bunch."

"And that would make sense," Pitt said. "Come on."

CHAPTER
FOURTEEN

The two of them struck boldly across the country, riding hard. At a headland, long later, Lex did not have to be told why Pitt pulled in his horse, rising in the stirrups to stare downward in hard attention, the life seeming to drain from his face. The distance below them was one of the ranch's main grazing areas. There should have been cattle in plenty down there, but none were in sight. The emptiness was a desolate eloquence.

"Maybe Holly just moved the steers somewhere else," Lex said in a tight voice.

"Or somebody else moved them."

They went down the slope at breakneck speed. Soon Lex was aware that it was a downed horse that they could now see ahead of them. They thundered up to it, two tense, unbelieving men. The horse had been shot through the head but was not out of the Toadstool band. Its brand was the dot-in-a-diamond of Bugeye, a shady shoestring outfit on the back edge of Slick Ear Plateau.

"Chess Turpin's spread," Pitt breathed. "Lex, we guessed it right, and I'm scared — damned scared."

The rider of the dead horse was not in evidence and had either walked away or been carried. Lex rode with a horrible dread. This evidence indicated that the herd had been fought for hotly, and now they had come upon signs that it had been shoved west in gathering speed that had mounted finally to a full run. Holly and his men must have done that crowding, preferring to scatter the steers down the basin to letting them be pushed the other way into the *mal país*. But where were the boys now?

Ahead loomed the shape of another stricken horse, the motionless heap that meant another rider had met with disaster. This time it was a Toadstool horse, its rider with it, and the rider was Holly. His leg was caught under the horse, twisted grotesquely, obviously crushed and broken and holding him helpless. But he was alive, and he stared at the newcomers with burning eyes.

"Know who it was, kid?" Lex asked tightly as he swung down.

"Don't ask me. It come so fast and furious, I don't know what went on. I tried to get the herd started toward the basin. Then my horse went down and caught me under it. All I could do afterward was lay here and listen. But there must have been eight or ten of them, and they come in shooting."

"Take it easy, and we'll see if we can get you out of there."

Pitt dismounted. Holly's leg was caught in the stirrup, Lex found, and was probably broken at the knee. The horse's barrel lay across it. Holly must have been pinned there for two or three hours, and the

156

ground about him showed where his fingers had dug in as he tried to pull himself loose.

Pitt looked at Lex privately in a grimace of despair. The two of them could not lift the dead weight of the horse and still pull Holly free. But the westward distance was empty of cattle and of riders who might help them. There were dots on the ground, without identity from this position, that could be men or horses or trampled steers.

The dead horse pinning down Holly had stiffened somewhat, and they began to turn this to their advantage. They used the saddles from their own mounts as props. Pitt and Lex joined strength to lift the animal by its hindquarters, straining until their faces twisted out of shape, while Holly managed to work the saddles farther in with each new gain.

Finally Holly groaned, "Think I'd come clear if somebody gave me a pull now."

At last they had him stretched out on the warming earth. Not until then did he let go, his eyes slowly closing and his body going slack. The break was just below the knee, which relieved Lex since it was less apt to be crippling. But a deeper fear was lessened somewhat when he observed the condition of the lower leg. From its appearance, circulation had not been shut off completely, reducing the danger of gangrene that could have cost Holly the whole limb.

"You go down and get the buckboard," Lex told Pitt. "Bring something to use as a splint, and you'd better bring some of the boys. While you're gone, I'll try and find out what lays west of here."

Pitt nodded, and they resaddled their horses. Pitt rode off at once, heading for ranch headquarters. Lex dropped Holly's hat over his eyes to protect him from the warming sun. For a moment he simply looked down at his brother, remembering that stoic, stubborn and lonely struggle under the weight of the horse. An affection he had not felt in a long while arose in him, then he swung up to the saddle.

He soon came upon Chuck Belton, who must have been knocked dead from the saddle for there was no horse thereabouts. Lex swung down, by then chilled too deeply for emotion. The rider was beyond help. Remounting, he rode on. Man by man in the next mile the whole sickening tally was made. There were outlaws mixed in now, but every man Holly had brought out to guard the herd had been killed in the long, running fight for the cattle.

Suddenly Lex grew aware of a party of horsemen in the forward distance. His hand dropped grimly to the grips of his gun and he kept place. His failure to take flight caused somebody to wave a hat above his head, the universal gesture of friendliness. But Lex knew by then that they could not be survivors of Holly's crew — there were none besides Holly. He waited warily.

As they rode nearer, coming on boldly, he eased. It was Ralph Turngate, ramrod of the big syndicate spread that lay west of Toadstool. The five punchers with him worked for that spread.

Turngate stared at Lex out of baffled eyes and said, "What the hell busted loose? A good part of your herd's piled itself halfway across our range."

158

Lex told them, watching his horror, his bitter anger, heat their faces.

"Well," Turngate said finally, "your boys sure tried, and my hat's off to every last man. But the rustlers must have made a pretty big cut on you, even so. What we seen, coming over, don't begin to account for your whole herd."

"The whole Slick Ear country must have been in on it!" a puncher exploded. "Enough of them to make sure they got their take! I guess we know what that means. That rat's nest has got to be wiped out. And a pity we didn't do it sooner."

"It's Toadstool's job," Lex said. "But I reckon we'll need help."

"And you'll sure get it," Turngate said promptly. "I'm not only speaking for myself. I know I can talk for the rest of the basin, too."

Lex nodded, aware that what he said would be a declaration of a war whose proportions he could not estimate, whose course he could not control.

He said, "Thanks, Ralph. We've got some sad chores to do — and then we'll talk it over."

Turngate and his men wanted to go on to Toadstool, and their help was needed. A man dropped off to wait with Holly until the buckboard could get there. Lifting the hat, Lex saw that Holly was still out of it, and that was merciful. The rest of them rode on in to headquarters.

Daylight revealed strong evidence of the night's violence. The dead and wounded had been removed, but empty cartridges were strewn everywhere, and

159

there wasn't a sound window pane left on the yard side of the house. Lex learned that a rider had departed right after daylight to bring Doc Cornell out from Flat Rock and remembered then that the doctor had been called out to the nester colony the night before. The buckboard came in with Holly, but the four hurt men had to wait for more than emergency attention . . .

It was Amy who arrived at Toadstool, around noon, rather than Doc Cornell. Lex met her in the yard and, without preamble, she said in a tired, tight voice, "Doc is still gone somewhere, Lex — he didn't come back all night! The worst of it is, I didn't recognize the nester who came for him so we could check up! Alf came to the house when he couldn't find him. He was so beat up, Big John made him turn in to sleep a while. But he thought I should come out and tell you about Doc — he's as worried as I am."

"Sometimes a case keeps Doc away a day or two, Amy," Lex said, feeling less confident than he tried to sound. "We've got to trust that's all there is to it, this time. Even if we're wrong, Doc's a pretty good man when it comes to taking care of himself."

"I hope you're right," she said. "Where's Holly?"

"In his bedroom in the house."

She swung down and ran up the steps. He took her horse on to the day corral, off-saddled and turned it in. Then he followed her indoors to find that she had gone at once to Holly's room. He continued on as far as that doorway, where he halted abruptly.

Amy had seated herself on the edge of Holly's bed, and the palm of her hand still touched his cheek. It was the look on both their faces that held Lex in arrest, for Amy's expression was more than sympathy for a friend who was hurt and in great pain. *If she ever doubted, she knows now*, Lex told himself. And maybe she had never doubted but only played him against Holly to make him come to taw. Lex retreated, still without having been observed.

Pitt, Turngate and two of Turngate's riders had left in midmorning to try to discover how many cattle the rustlers had managed to pick up on Starlight range and where they had drifted them. The four men were back soon after Amy's arrival and called Lex into conference at once.

"There's no way to make a close estimate," Pitt reported, "but the sons had help aplenty. There's sign that they managed to round up several hefty bunches and drift 'em northeast."

Lex said, "Any chance to head them off?"

"The way I look at it," Pitt said, "we've got plenty of time. That Slick Ear bunch has always whittled on the basin. Blotting brands and mixing the stuff into their own herds. And I think that's all they figure on this time, relying on Conbuck not to give them too much trouble. It ain't like the old days. It's got pretty hard to get a big hot herd out of the country and to find a market willing to risk buying it."

Lex nodded. "I reckon you're right. But we've got to jump 'em before they split up."

"I think they'll blot the brands before they start cutting, Lex. You can tell that from the way they drifted. They're going into one of them backland meadows. But we don't dare give 'em much leeway. Ralph and me decided to come in and get organized for maybe tonight."

Turngate nodded. "To say nothing of you boys getting some sleep beforehand. Me, I don't hanker to go into a battle with a bunch of hombres who can't keep their eyes open. You get at that. I'll see the rest of the basiners and have 'em collect here right after dark. That all right?"

"If you're right about it being safe to wait that long."

Lex climbed the stairs to the bedroom he used at the ranch, feeling that rest was impossible but knowing that Turngate was right about it. He pulled off his boots and stretched out on the bed, irritable and restless as an aftermath of violence, which was aggravated by the day's full heat. He tried to recall how long it had been since he had slept soundly or eaten much but could not. But the sheer weight of exhaustion began to have its way, and at last he drowsed.

He did not know how long he had lain so when he opened his eyes to find Amy bending over him, shaking him gently.

She said, "I hate to wake you up — but Frank Renwick's downstairs. He insists on seeing you right now."

"Renwick? What's he want to do — write up the massacre for his newspaper?"

"I think you'd better see him," Amy said, and slipped out.

He rose, pulled on his boots and went groggily down the stairs. Amy had let Renwick into the little ranch office, where Lex found the man pacing the floor. A look of sullenness on the editor's face lay deeper than his obvious embarrassment.

"Surprised, Lex?" Renwick asked. He moved over behind Lex and himself closed the door.

"You've got a nerve coming here, man. What brings you?"

"To start off with, let me assure you that I came on my own initiative."

"You've got such a faculty?"

"All right — rub it in." Temper flashed in Renwick's eyes, but he managed to keep his outward manner casual. "You and I could strike a mighty convenient bargain right now, Lex. That's what I came to talk about."

"Me bargain with you?"

"You might not find it so unattractive if you'll hear what I want to say to you."

"All right. Set down and start talking."

"I'm too damned restless to sit still. I'm here because I want to break with Staff Palgrave. I need your help to do it. If you give it, I think I can throw you the advantage you need. I'm sure I can tell you things that will save a lot of trouble — and a lot more bloodshed. This I want you to know. I haven't sanctioned a one of the killings that have been done or tried."

Lex's eyes were narrowed, cold. "I get a set of Palgrave's blueprints if I agree to help you in advance — is that it?"

Renwick shook his head. "No. I'll tell you those plans because they're what I think will persuade you to help me."

"Help you in what way?"

"Simply endorse me after I've broken clean with Palgrave. Until you replace Tom Lerner, there's nobody running against me personally."

"Being a dinky county commissioner means enough to you that you're willing to give up all the profits that come through Palgrave? You've printed better jokes than that in your newspaper, Renwick. You've got a hidden motive — or you're scared of Palgrave, yourself."

"All right — I'm scared of Palgrave, myself. I'm sick of licking his hand, and I can't take the belittling, the contemptuous way he treats me. He knows it, that I'm becoming dangerous to him. The same as Hap Haber is. I've got a feeling that I'm going to be eliminated, along with the rest."

"What rest, man?"

"All his political enemies — all the men dangerous to him. His whole play is to create a state of anarchy in the county so he can do that without it being too apparent."

"Then," Lex said on a slow breath, "Doc Cornell's already in trouble."

"I don't know anything about Cornell. Palgrave and Conbuck are running the show now. I haven't been in on their talk for several days. Conbuck likes it that way. He's a lick-spittle, and I know he's had a lot to do with getting me dealt out of it. But I was in on the basic plan, and it has gone too far to be changed. They've armed the nesters heavily. The original intention was to start up that old war again. It jumped the track when Tom Lerner proved to be smarter than they estimated. Now I don't know."

"Haber hit us, last night. They made a cut of Toadstool cattle."

"Haber probably did it on his own, then. He's got his hooks in Palgrave and Conbuck both. He hasn't been satisfied with his share of the profits. Like me, I think Hap Haber is going to get eliminated."

"What's your particular plan?" Lex asked.

"What I said. I'll withdraw from the political race, declaring I can't stomach what I've seen going on. Then I want you to congratulate me and urge that I go on as one of the clean-up candidates."

Lex shook his head. "No go, Renwick. You never started reforming till you started losing out."

"It may be your life — Cornell's — John Starlight's, too."

"We know that, and so far we've stayed alive. Too bad about you, man, but you made your own bed."

Renwick's voice turned deadly then. "So — I'll have to play out my string. I haven't told you too much yet that you didn't know. I could have given you some real help."

"I reckon we'll have to do it the hard way, then. You better go now, Renwick. The boys out here are in the mood to string up a machine man about now."

"My offer stands, if you change your mind."

Lex said nothing, watching the man swing out through the door. He had felt a strong temptation to see what he could worm out of Renwick about Abel and Sara Jerome, but it had been too hard a subject to broach. Then a more immediate thing rose to fill his mind, his worry about Doc Cornell.

It struck him that there was a chance of learning who was sick or hurt among the nesters from Rita Lerner. He sought out Pitt at once to say, "You see Renwick here?"

"Yeah. He just drop in to pay his regards?"

"A hell of a lot more than that." Lex gave him the gist of what had passed between himself and Renwick, saying in conclusion, "It's made me sick with concern for Doc. I'm going over to see if Rita Lerner can throw any light at all on where Doc is and what's holding him up. We've got men here who need him bad. Doc would have come along if he had any idea of what we had happen."

"Turngate's calling the basiners here for a meeting tonight, you know," Pitt said.

"Let 'em have it. But don't you move out on anything at all until I get back. I'm scared, man. We've got to know what we're doing."

"I put you there, Lex, and I'll try to hold 'em back till you come."

CHAPTER
FIFTEEN

Although he found the food tasteless, Lex forced himself to eat a full meal before he saddled up. He rode out quietly, with Pitt the only one aware of his intentions. By then, evening's long shadows had begun to stretch out from the hills. As it lost its full brightness, the sky softened to a deep and mellow blue. The day's heat declined.

By the time he had picked his way through the many runs of the breaks, the sun hung in full flame on the western rim of the hills. He was by then on the headland above the nester flat, and he had barely looked upon that wheeling plain when he pulled down his horse in abrupt attention.

A party of nearly a dozen horsemen rode toward him. The mounts were not the heavy, lumbering animals of the farming gentry, but that fact was not the main interest in what he saw. Sunlight splintered on several vests to declare the identity of these men.

Conbuck, he thought, and the sheriff was afield in force, himself and deputies evidenced by the polished badges of office they all liked to sport, with others drawn into the group apparently to form the whole. Curiosity as to why they were moving across the nester flats, coming toward the breaks, wiped out for the time being the other purposes in Lex's mind.

Looking about, he espied a lateral rim from which he could watch them long enough to learn more of their destination. Wheeling his horse about, he put it back along its own course until he came to a side run, where he cut sharply to the right. He was leaving fresh sign behind, which might not be a safe thing to do at the moment, but had no time to try to avoid that.

He reached a place presently where he could ride onto the bench from which he meant to keep tabs. He swung down, ground-tied the animal out of sight, then moved quietly back to a place where he could see a stretch of the main trail through the roughs. He was well ahead of the sheriff's party. But soon he picked up the vibration of hoofs coming against the earth. The riders were not hurrying. At last they strung out into view below him.

He saw at once that they had discerned his sign, with one man following it in interest. The whole party reined in at the lower end of the side run. They discussed something in soundless movements of mouth and lips and then rode on along the main trail. Either they were not worried about someone's having pulled back from them so hurriedly or were carried forward on their own track by some concern of their own.

Lex let them be swallowed by intervening obstructions, then swung back into saddle. A hunchlike excitement had risen in him. Conbuck apparently was entering the cattle basin, and it would have been much more convenient for him to have brought his party along the regular basin road. The stealth indicated that the venture might bear watching, that the movement was of importance to him and his allies.

He rode at a safe distance in the rear, with dusk beginning to thicken about him. The big party he followed seemed unswerving in its purpose and yet to be unrushed, otherwise. Then, with still enough light left to see plainly, he came upon another sudden puzzle. Conbuck had turned his men off the trail into the basin and into another run that pointed due north. Lex hesitated only for a moment, then continued his careful following.

Night came on so that he could no longer make out the sign easily as he rode. But he was certain that the party was still pressing onward toward its destination and by then he had begun to develop a clue as to what that destination could be. There was some wild back range on ahead, used by the denizens of the Slick Ear Plateau.

He soon had grown so confident that this movement had something to do with the cattle run off that day from Starlight range that he was tempted to cut around and get ahead of Conbuck's group. He got a chance, a few minutes later, which set his decision to try it. A rim break let him thread a narrow canyon to come upon a rubble slant mounting to a long bench. He got on top and was well enough over that he felt emboldened to lift his horse to a forward rush. He kept up that clip for ten minutes before the mesa ran out.

But it halted at the edge of one of the many grassed holes among the tangled hills. Out at a distance below him was the dwarfed light of a campfire. He swung down and seated himself at the head of his horse to stare at it, trying to discern its meaning. The Slick Ear contingent was well quartered and had no need to camp out. That led to a definite conclusion. This was a temporary cow camp. Excitement began to prick at the nape of his neck. It was two to one that, at this moment, he was not very far from a sizeable cut of Starlight cattle. The only puzzle was why Conbuck had chosen to visit it with such a force.

The only way to determine that was to wait and see what developed. He sat motionless, staring into the pale black of the night, his gaze riveted on the campfire. About him quiet seemed to rise out of the wildland to envelop and swallow him until at last he began to feel alone upon an empty world. As the minutes stretched on into what seemed an hour, he began to wonder if he had not misguessed the intentions and course of Conbuck's party, after all. Finally he indulged a long-denied desire to smoke and rolled a cigarette. He turned away from the campfire to light it quickly, and at that moment a far-off crack of a rifle rent the night.

He dropped the cigarette and ground it out in an angry reflex before the sudden outcrackling of many other guns informed him that he had had nothing to do with the shooting. Night now was a help to him and he could see the lacing of fire streaks go back and forth about the campfire and realized in bewilderment that the outlaw camp was under attack. Conbuck's big party had jumped it — there was no other explanation.

An unintentional observer, Lex lay flat on the headland, carefully holding onto the reins of his nervous horse. A furious assault had opened on the camp. Its probable out-guard had been overcome, and it had been caught in complete surprise. The pattern of development sent Lex's thoughts unerringly to his conversation with Frank Renwick that afternoon. The editor had expressed grim confidence that Hap Haber was due to feel the treacherous power of the machine he had served so faithfully and against which he had been growing restive.

A cool grin formed on Lex's lips, for Haber must be there in that besieged camp. Conbuck must have heard early that day, from the Toadstool rider who had gone to Flat Rock for the doctor, that Haber had hit Toadstool hard and without mercy. The sheriff had seized upon that excuse to carry out the purge upon the outlaw leader and his immediate supporters. It was ironical, Lex thought, to be sitting here and innocently watching somebody else give Haber what he so longed to give him, himself.

But, watching closely, he realized that Conbuck was not finding it an easy accomplishment. Hap Haber might have expected treachery, also, but had been forced out of common sense to expect trouble from Starlight Basin. So he must have been in force, too. Lex hoped that the two factions would prove mutually annihilating.

Slowly he realized that the returned shooting from positions about the campfire was diminishing. It was no wonder. The attackers had swiftly encompassed the

171

camp, laying upon it a wicked and unrelenting gunfire. Lex could already guess that Conbuck meant to take no prisoners back to town with him. There would be a number of dead rustlers, his special enemies among them, and a big cut of stolen cattle. Haber's private greed in carrying out a cattle raid had provided the Palgrave machine with a perfect excuse for its purge.

When the signs pointed more strongly to the fact that the vicious gunfight was nearing its end, Lex began to give thought to his own safety. He could do nothing one way or the other about what was taking place out there nor about the Toadstool cattle he believed to be in the immediate vicinity. Rising stiffly from his long wait, he swung about to the horse and went up into saddle.

He was soon down off the rim and coming into the larger run by which the sheriff's posse had entered the area. He trusted that the fighting had riveted attention upon the encircled camp and boldly entered the main run. He hadn't even lined out the horse again when somebody's voice ripped out through the night at him.

"Hey, there — who is it?"

Not recognizing the voice, Lex flattened and drove in his spurs. Too late he recalled how he had been obliged to let them learn of his own presence in the vicinity. In the excitement, he had failed to remember that Conbuck dared not risk a chance witness to what was taking place. So the man had left somebody here to intercept him if he heard the shooting and tried to work closer to its source.

A horse thundered out behind him and a gun spoke, a rifle. Lex felt a moment of wild alarm as he felt a

172

break in his own mount's stride. Abruptly it was caving out from under him, pitching up its hindquarters. He tried to throw himself free, and that was the last he knew . . .

He was first aware of voices about him, then of the hard, still warm earth under his back. In a swirl of roiled sensations, he could not at first make out what it was all about. Then he realized that he had been taken into the camp of the outlaws, which now was in the hands of the sheriff's posse. He stared about, seeing the legs and foreshortened bodies of several men. Instantly somebody noticed his movement and spoke to him.

"Well, Starlight, we got the jiggers who raided you. Too bad you weren't bright enough to declare yourself to my deputy. It would have saved you a mean spill."

Lex climbed to a tottering stand and for a long moment stared into the amused face of Conbuck. The fight over, they had refreshed the campfire and were drinking coffee, heated and victorious men who now regarded him with unconcealed animosity.

"And picked off a pretty neat prize of your own, didn't you?" Lex answered.

"Haber? I've been wanting to get something definite on that slick son for a long while. This time I did. He's over there dead, along with five of his sidekicks."

"Never took one live prisoner?" Lex asked in mock surprise.

"They were up against a hanging charge," Conbuck pointed out. "Every last man of them fought till he was killed."

"How will you work it when it comes to Renwick, Conbuck? And would you by any chance know why Doc Cornell's been kept out of town so long?"

"What do you mean by that reference to Renwick, man?" Conbuck asked narrowly.

"He come to see me today. Tried to double-cross you and Palgrave — the way you did Haber. I don't mind telling you that, nor if you sweat him plenty about it."

"Don't you worry about Frank Renwick."

"I'm not. But I am worried about Doc."

"And maybe about yourself?"

"From what Renwick said about this whole thing being a smokescreen for getting rid of Palgrave's enemies, I've got reason to wonder about myself. But you can't beef me here and claim I was one of the rustlers. Not with Toadstool cattle the cause of it all. So what's it going to be — you figure on trying to press through the claim that it was me who murdered Tom Lerner?"

"Too slow — and too risky," Conbuck said with finality. "We'll leave the dead and departed and send out a wagon tomorrow. Somebody catch a Haber horse for Starlight, here. He's going with us."

Soon Lex found himself riding in the midst of a large group of determined men and realized he was not going to be successful, this time, in breaking away. His head still roared in pain, and his left shoulder was sore and stiff from its recent impact against the hard ground. Conbuck led them and pointed the way back along the route by which the breaks had been threaded

174

coming in. The sheriff rode with an arrogant confidence.

When at last they came down upon the nester flat, the party abruptly broke in two. Lex found himself riding with a pair of men, who bent their course at a full turn to the left, striking out across the flat. He had heard no orders passed, but the pair seemed to be fully instructed. They cut the main road serving the flat and there turned left once again. A half hour after that they were riding in toward one of the flimsier nester shacks on the edge of the colony.

A dog let loose in sudden racket and was cursed silent by somebody at the place. One of Lex's companions called out, "It's all right, Elvie — it's us." Then they rode up on the drab little place, which consisted of the shack and an equally haphazard barn. The door of the house was open, a man standing there with a rifle in plain evidence. He took a long look at the new arrivals before he relaxed his vigilance.

"You pull it off?" he asked.

"We sure did, Elvie."

"Who's he, then, and what's he doing here? I thought Conbuck said there wasn't going to be a one left alive. We meant what we said, Durham. You boys have got to cover every track if you want us nesters to string along with you."

"Don't worry about that. This is Lex Starlight — as big a haul as we've made since you boys helped us suck in Doc Cornell. And both are twice as big a fish as Hap Haber."

"What you going to do with him?"

"Deal him out of this game whether he likes it or don't. Couldn't you guess that, Elvie?"

"I dunno . . ." the nester said doubtfully, then shrugged. "Well — come on in. But I don't mind telling you I'm leery of holding 'em here alive."

"Elvie, shut up," Durham said sharply.

But the nester's ill-concealed apprehension had sent a bolt of energy through Lex. The gravity of his position had been made painfully plain by the swift, ruthless way in which Hap Haber had been wiped out. Though stringing along, this nester had been rendered uneasy about that kind of treachery. If Haber had been destroyed once his usefulness was over, no other man serving the machine even temporarily could dismiss the chance of the same fate for himself.

And the man had spoken in the plural in his reference to prisoners. That brought hope boiling up in Lex. If Doc Cornell had fallen into the hands of his enemies, he was at or somewhere near this place. If so, Lex reflected, his own mischance might turn out to be a stroke of luck.

Durham swung down from the saddle and motioned roughly to Lex, who followed suit. The nester vanished into the inner darkness, then the flickering light of a dirty lamp destroyed some of the gloomy atmosphere. Recovered from the effects of his hard fall with the shot horse, Lex felt a cool, competitive excitement course through his veins. He had unearthed more about Doc Cornell than he could have gained from Rita Lerner. His impulse in following Conbuck's party had not thrown him off the track as badly as he had supposed at first. Now he had the same strong hunch that he was close to the goal he sought.

Lex looked about with distaste. It was obvious that the sodbuster bached here and was of the riffraff breed that likewise hung on the outer fringe of the cattle settlements. He was young, burly and possessed of an irritable sort of diffidence.

The habitation was a one-room affair, all the sorry living being done in a single and sloppy space. There was a front and back door, and two small windows in the front wall. The spare furniture was crude, homemade, and scattered haphazardly about. There certainly was no evidence of Cornell's presence, but that back door interested Lex more than he let himself reveal. He hoped he was going to be left alone here in Elvie's surly care.

The next few minutes showed him that, if fortune had smiled upon him at all, it had changed its mood. Durham's tight-lipped saddlemate made some quick disposition of the horses and came indoors. In a gruff, overbearing way, Durham said, "We could use a bait of grub, Elvie," and seated himself in the room's best chair to be catered to. The nameless man, who seemed to dislike attention, planted his gluteals on the edge of a bunk in a corner free of light.

Elvie, increasingly unhappy about the situation, rattled the stovelids and began to lay a fire.

Giving him a flat stare, Lex said, "How long's it going to be before you get a slug in the belly, Elvie? Right now you're useful to Palgrave and Conbuck, but you won't be very long. You going to sleep sound nights, after that?"

"Mebbe you ought to button your lip, Starlight," Durham said.

Lex grinned coolly. "Just the same, Elvie's doing a lot of thinking along that line. Aren't you, Elvie? You know you stand in more danger from that direction than from holding Cornell and me prisoner on your place and maybe letting us be murdered here."

"Who said anything about Cornell being here?" Durham asked quickly.

"By God, he's right!" the nester exploded. "What happens to me and the other boys after this thing's run its course?"

"All right, Sid," Durham said mildly. "We knew we'd have it to do."

Lex was even less prepared than Elvie for what happened. The shack's small space jarred abruptly to the explosion of a gun. Elvie had lacked the time to turn fully toward this Sid. But Lex swung in cold fury to see the six-gun in the killer's fist. Sid had not risen from his seat, and his face was without expression. The nester staggered, then came down in a lifeless heap on the floor.

"All right, you got him killed off, Starlight," Durham drawled. "But it never helped you any."

"So there's Tom Lerner's murderer," Lex returned, still staring at Sid. "I figured it was Hap Haber. But I don't think even he could have gunned down a man as cool as that. Do I get mine now?"

"Not yet. You've guessed pretty close, and there's no sense beating around the bush. Cornell's here. So's Tom Lerner's widder. But none of you three can be killed off and left to the buzzards. Don't take too much comfort from that, though. There'll be a situation along where things'll be right for getting rid of all of you."

"The big range war? You really think you can get the nesters to follow you in one?"

Durham grinned. "There's one thing about the nesters. They stick together when they're under fire. You've seen that happen. If they're attacked, they'll fight as one man."

"You'll have to cut the deck deeper than that if you want me to get the drift."

"It's your side that'll start the war, Starlight." Durham's grin was mocking, serene. "I'm a pig's uncle if it ain't under way already after what Haber done to your crew."

"Maybe," Lex admitted. "But that had nothing to do with the nester flat."

"So far, buck. But if some nesters beef Cornell or Lex Starlight, with Haber dead and gone, then it's going to be the nester colony that gets scotched. Ain't it now, Starlight?"

CHAPTER
SIXTEEN

In a flat, deadly voice, Sid the gunman said, "Durham, you've got more tongue than brains. You better do something about that carcass on the floor before it gets you into trouble."

"We've got to see Conbuck, first."

"Get him out of sight, man, before whoever it is that's coming gets here."

Lex straightened, listening intently. Like Durham's, his ears lacked the furtive keenness of the outlaw's. But in the sudden stillness he could detect the hoof falls of a swiftly moving horse. Alarm leaped onto the face of Durham then, for none could foretell who it was.

Sid said, "Turn down the light, Durham, but don't blow it out. Man's seen it by now, and I aim to keep my eyes on this Starlight rooster." He sat still, leaving it up to the frightened deputy to prepare for the unexpected visitor.

Cursing, Durham bent and struggled up, getting the slack body of Elvie across his shoulder. He looked about the room, then moved toward the door and lurched out into the darkness.

"A punk," Sid said, thinly amused. "For what it's worth to you, Starlight, I'd peg you for twice the man.

Your kind wouldn't be lickin' the boots of any badge-toter like Conbuck."

"Thanks," Lex said. "I also doubt that I could shoot a helpless man the way you just did Elvie."

"My job, buck. What I get paid for."

"Be the same if Elvie'd had a gun and a fair shake?"

Sid shook his head. "No. For that I'd want twice the money."

Durham was back at once, having made some hurried disposition of the body. The beat of hoofs was closer, unmistakably coming in on the shack. Lex felt his mouth go dry, for if it was either another machine man or another nester his position would not be helped. Then the horse stopped just outdoors and a voice bawled out.

"Hey, Elvie!"

"You better be polite, Durham," Sid warned.

Durham opened the door, saying, "Elvie ain't here, this evening. Oh — it's you, Louie. What's on your mind?"

"Plenty. Where's Elvie?"

"Be damned if I know, Louie. We been waiting for him, ourselves."

"By God, you hyenas have got some questions to answer, and the answers had better sound right!"

There was a pause, then Durham stepped back before the hostile advance of a tall, thin man with dark whiskers and hair. Lex stared at him, recognizing Louie Andrea, the hot-headed brother of Rita Lerner. Then Andrea gave him the same quick, jolted look of recognition.

"What in hell are you doing here, Starlight?" he demanded.

Lex shrugged and tipped his head toward Durham. "Ask him." A warning bell had sounded deep in his mind. If he said too much he would endanger Andrea, and the two gun-hawks were relying on him to realize that fact.

Suspicion had already risen on the settler's face, and under it was a deep concern.

"Something's fishy — mighty so," he said. "Last night Elvie come and told my sister that Mamie Tronson was sick again and wanted her to come and help. I never gave it another thought till tonight when Rita didn't come home or send word. So I went to Tronson's. Mamie never sent for Rita — she ain't even sick. Something's wrong. Elvie lied, and I aim to get to the bottom of it."

"Maybe he got the names mixed up," Durham said mildly. "Slip of the tongue, him meaning some other woman. He must be there, too. Anyhow, he ain't around here anywhere. Sorry we can't help you, Louie."

"What's that?"

Andrea's gaze had strayed to a dark patch on the floor where Elvie had fallen. Durham tried to cover it with his own shadow. "By God, Durham," Andrea rapped, "that's blood!"

"Easy, Louie . . ."

"Whose is it — Elvie's? Say — what's going on here?"

182

A cold, sick dread was in Lex, for he fully expected to see that quick, cruel gun rise in Sid's fist. Durham stood flabbergasted but Sid, with a cold grin, took up the talk.

"There was a ruckus up in the hills, this evening," he said. "I got a slug in my leg, and it wouldn't be healthy for me to see a sawbones to get it dug out. There's a little demand for me, here and there. So I made Durham do it, and he like to have butchered me he's so goddam clumsy with his hands. That right, Starlight?"

"That's right," Lex said and tried to sound convincing.

"Well, I dunno . . ." Then Andrea shrugged. Maybe he had swallowed that or maybe he had begun to realize his own mounting peril. He was lost in deep thought for a moment, then he said, "Well, if it ain't Mamie's doing sending for Rita, I don't know who it could have been."

"Must have been Elvie got his tongue twisted, all right," Lex offered, determined to save the man from his own temper and worry. "I heard Doc Cornell was called out this way last night, too. We needed him on Toadstool and sent a man to town, and that's what we heard."

Without another word, Andrea walked out.

"He never fell for that," Durham said uneasily. "Sid, we got to move outta here."

"Where to?"

"Into the hills."

"I get enough of that the way it is."

"What if he'd insisted on taking a look around the place?"

"Then I'd have took care of him."

"You better think twice about that, buck," Durham spat. "Elvie's scum and the nesters know it. But when it comes to Andrea, he's of another cut. It wouldn't be smart for something to happen to him and his sister both. We got to get outta here. He's apt to be back, and when he's sure he's had dust throwed in his eyes, he might bring help."

"Mebbeso," Sid said finally. "All right, Starlight — start walking. Your amigos are locked up in Elvie's excuse of a barn. Hog-tied and gagged to boot, and I doubt that Durham can get them in shape to fork horses very quick. But I reckon he was right about that Andrea hombre. Struck me he could be hell on red wheels, the same as you — which is an impression I just don't seem to get from Durham except when he's top dog and knows it beyond mistake."

Lex suffered himself to be marched outdoors and down to the barn. Somewhere deep in his brain flickered a thin flame of hope. United with Cornell and the Lerner woman, he would be in a far better position to act if a chance appeared. Some kind usually did — if a man was willing to accept long odds.

The three saddle horses, ridden into the place by himself and his two guards, had been turned into what looked like a corral for milk cows alongside the barn. Sid kept his gun on Lex while Durham roped and saddled the animals. Then Durham ventured into the dark barn and presently brought out two more horses. One of them was Cornell's fine saddler, the other the type of plug a nester woman might ride. Durham went

184

back inside again and was longer, that time, in reappearing.

But two figures staggered before him, a man's and a woman's. Cornell swung his head about numbly, then his attention fixed on Lex.

"What are you doing here?" he gasped.

"Same as you and Missus Lerner, Doc, except I wasn't tricked. I was just careless enough to let these sons get the jump on me."

"Get aboard," Durham said uneasily, "and let's get outta here."

"You all right, Missus Lerner?" Lex insisted.

"Except that I can hardly move."

"And you, Doc?"

"Except for being mauled a little. When I discovered what I'd walked into, I gave them something of a fight."

"Shut up and get onto them horses," Sid snapped.

Both Cornell and the woman had to be helped up. Afterward Durham led the way, Sid and his deadly gun coming behind the party. Durham struck out at once for the benighted hills in the western distance. Riding three abreast so that Sid could watch each one, Lex had his eye on a screen of softwood trees just ahead, lying along some small water-course. Hope was all but dead in him by then. He might make some kind of quick, desperate move, but it would only bring disaster to one of his friends.

As if aware that the approaching brush might tempt him to try something, Durham bent abruptly to the right, skirting the trees a hundred yards out. But the party had scarcely lined out on its new tack when sound, startlingly unexpected, rent the night. From somewhere in the brush, a rifle cracked out.

Lex didn't know what it was, but he heard Sid grunt behind him. In the next instant, exultant that he had been so on the alert himself, he swung his horse in a swift, blunt jump at Durham's. The man had turned his own mount half around, jerking up his gun and searching the hostile brush with frantic eyes. That mechanical reaction gave Lex his chance, and the two horses came together with a tremendous crash. Sending himself with a driving thrust of his legs, Lex catapulted forward and caught hold of Durham and they spilled to the earth together.

He was aware of one supreme fact — that there was no more shooting. Therefore that first shot had drilled into Sid. Enheartened, Lex fought off the impact of the crash to the ground. He had hold of Durham's throat and he rolled on top and put his last strength into his hands. The jolt had stilled Durham to a groggy, twisting struggle. That stopped, and still Lex held on.

Then Doc Cornell's voice was saying, "That's enough, Lex. He's quit. And whoever it was who fired that shot — he got the gunman through the head."

"Ten to one it was Louie Andrea," Lex panted.

Then a horse broke out of the trees and came forward, a heavy animal. Rita Lerner gave out a small, glad cry of recognition as she saw her brother on it. Andrea still held his rifle cautiously as he rode up, and Lex realized he still was not sure how Lex Starlight stood in the situation.

"Come on, Louie," Lex called. "I was as helpless as Doc and your sister back there."

Andrea rode on in. Swinging down, he took a long look at Sid. "Sure didn't like to drill a man without warning," he said. "But that was the only way I could be sure he didn't get one of you."

"I didn't figure they'd fooled you much," Lex said.

"And I seen I'd scared that ratty Durham plenty. So I decided to hang around and see if they rabbitted. Figured if they did it would be toward the hills, and I didn't have much trouble getting in ahead of you. What in tunket was it all about, anyhow, Rita?"

"I just don't know, Louie," the woman answered.

"Well, I do," Lex said grimly. "You smarter nesters must have figured out by now that Palgrave wants to start up the old war between our side and yours. Tom Lerner was too level-headed to let it come off the first time they tried to start it. Meanwhile Palgrave got rid of some personal enemies and pests. But he wanted a better smokescreen before he went after the big ones. You, Doc, and Tom's wife were picked to be the victims of some kind of a staged outrage to get both sides heated up past holding. I don't know just how — and it don't matter if we play it smart from here on."

"They murdered Elvie?" Andrea asked.

"Yes, but it was like you suspected. He was helping them right down the line. He didn't get scrupulous but scared, and that's what cost him his life. As for you, Louie, I think you and your sister better come stay at Toadstool till this thing's settled."

"No," Rita Lerner said promptly. "We don't want protection, and we won't be fooled again. Palgrave's got lots of support amongst the farmers. It's our duty to see as many of them as we can and see that they hear the straight of things."

Lex touched his hat, saying, "Ma'am, I was brought up to despise nesters. But from what I've seen of you, your husband and your brother, I'll go to bat for you any time."

"You just see that your side uses sense, Starlight," Andrea answered. "You know we got our grudges, too, and we ain't had too much consideration from you cowmen. We only knocked one of Palgrave's capers in the head, and the man's got a hatful. This one would have brought what he wants, and the next one still might. What do we do about them two shytpokes on the ground, there?"

"It's the first time in my life," Cornell said, "that I've been happy to pronounce a man dead. But both of them are, and good riddance. Under the circumstances, I think we'd better just leave them. Somebody's bound to check at Elvie's, then scout around and find 'em. Meanwhile, we'd better all get out of here."

They parted, Andrea and his sister riding off to the southeast. For a long moment Lex stared after them.

"Time's come to clean this country up, Doc," he said, "and give everybody a fresh and decent start."

"That's what the election's all about, son."

"Doc — that won't do it. You must know that after what you've been through."

Cornell let out a long sigh. "Yes, I guess I do. And hate it. But I think Palgrave realizes that, at long last, he would be licked at the polls. So he doesn't mean to let it be decided that way, himself. We'd best accept the situation."

They rode out at once, pointing for the breaks and far-off Toadstool. In spite of all that had happened since he left ranch headquarters, Lex figured from the stars that it was not much past midnight. He was remembering that Ralph Turngate had been going to call a meeting of the basiners at Toadstool, and he wondered what decisions had been reached and if the men were still there.

He hoped so, for he was slowly forming his own plan of attack on the machine now that open war was inevitable. One thing he knew. It would be costly and so had to be cautious and yet conclusive. What he had seen and learned tonight had been horror piled on brazen horror. The thought led his mind unavoidably to Sara Jerome, who must have had a part in the thing, however small, however unknowing of its full color and significance.

He said, "Doc, have you ever formed an opinion of Abel Jerome?"

"I've seen very little of him."

"Well, it keeps hitting me over and over that I've seen him somewhere before. But I'm damned if I can place it. I haven't told anybody yet, but I've run into pretty strong evidence that he's been working for Palgrave on the quiet. Yet parts of it just don't add up that way."

"The pretty part?" Cornell asked with a dry chuckle.

"All right — I guess I just hate to look at the truth of it."

"I always thought it was you and Amy."

"I guess it's Amy and Holly, Doc — and I reckon that suits me fine. Which sure leaves me high and dry, don't it?"

"Well, you were once wrong about the Lerners, you know," Doc said, and after that they fell quiet.

CHAPTER
SEVENTEEN

When Lex rode in on the Toadstool ranchhouse, its windows were dark save for one where a single lamp burned. He was thinking now of Holly and his long-unattended leg, as well as the wounded men in the bunkhouse. The fact that Cornell could now give them his help was more important at the moment than the meeting that must have broken up with its purpose unfulfilled.

Cornell swung down from his saddle, a tired, worn man but a physician to the marrow. His saddlebags contained his medicines and instruments. He removed them and, with the bags slung across stooped shoulders, slowly mounted the steps to the house.

Lex took the horses on to the corral. A puncher appeared in the doorway of the bunkhouse, which also showed a shaded light.

"I got Doc," Lex said. "He'll take care of things fast."

"Man, am I glad to hear that. These boys have been catching hell."

When he had put up the horses, Lex went at once to the big house. Pitt Berts met him in the hallway. "Doc and Amy have started in on Holly," he reported. "Said that they'd call on us if necessary and otherwise we should keep out of the way. Doc looks like he's had trouble, himself. Where'd you find him?"

Lex explained.

"By God," Pitt said, at the conclusion, "it looks like we've got to settle things with that nester flat along with the machine."

"That's not the answer. Elvie paid for his little ambitions, whatever they were. Probably others have lent his brand of help, too. Then there's a fair-sized contingent that figures it does better under Palgrave than it would stringing along with us. But there's also quite a few nesters, Pitt, cut to the pattern of Louie Andrea and Rita Lerner."

"You should have heard the talk at the meeting tonight," Pitt returned. "They figure that what supports the machine is as bad as the machine, itself."

"If we start squabbling with the nesters, it'll be just what Palgrave wants." Lex's voice grew more gentle in tone. Pitt was the kind of ramrod who developed affection and a deep sense of responsibility toward his men. That caused them, in turn, to give him their undying loyalty. Pitt had seen too many of those boys die in wanton, cold-blooded slaughter to be charitable toward even the associates of the Palgrave machine, however innocent they might have been of evil intentions.

"I reckon," Pitt said with a tired sigh. "But it's hard to set on your hands, Lex — mighty hard. The basiners will all be back tomorrow night. I promised them that by then we could give 'em something they can get their teeth into. Meanwhile, I reckon we better bring in them steers you found on the plateau."

"A good idea. A man working is a lot steadier than one round-siding it idle."

It was not long until Doc Cornell emerged from Holly's room. He went at once to the bunkhouse, Pitt accompanying him. Lex went in to see Holly who, with his leg in a splint and his pain eased by an opiate, was able to grin at him.

"Doc tells me you had a busy night," he said to Lex.

"Well, it sure didn't seem dull. He figure you'll be able to use that peg of yours again?"

It was Amy who nodded in answer. Her face was worn, showing the strain of her constant vigil but now overlaid with relief.

"The break's below the knee. It was hard to set after going so long, but this man didn't let a peep out of him. Doc says that with that kind of spirit, Holly will be able to get around as good as ever in a few weeks."

"As if a few weeks was no time at all," Holly said with a groan.

"You're lucky," Lex retorted.

"Lex, I am. I got to tell you something. Amy and me mean to be married as soon as the trouble's cleared up."

"I'm glad to hear it," Lex said, finding it easy and seeing relief surge into their eyes. He turned and went out.

Somewhere a pain had started in him. It was not regret at losing Amy to Holly. There were no two people on earth he would rather see team up. It was, rather, a sudden insight into the depth of the feeling he had conceived for Sara without understanding it at the time. Somehow those long minutes of fusion in the Jerome barn, her reluctance, her ensuing impetuosity, her final outpouring of her love seemed as real, as sincere as the feeling he could now see plainly between Amy and Holly. He could not believe that there had been pretense and hidden design in the woman who had given herself to him so fully. And yet every dictate of a realistic mind told him that there must have been.

Lex was waiting in the little ranch office when Pitt returned from the bunkhouse.

"Well everybody's fixed up," Pitt said. "And Doc's turned in at the bunkhouse. Lex, what are we going to tell the basiners when they get here the next time? They're set for war, and they don't care much who they carry it to."

"I don't reckon they'll want to hand things to Palgrave on a platter."

"You got a way around that?"

Lex rolled a cigarette and lighted it thoughtfully. "Maybe. I'll put it up to you and them and let you all decide. You remember that, right after Tom Lerner was murdered, Doc served warning to the country that if things got too dirty he'd ask the state to step in. Palgrave's crowded the situation so close to the anarchy he's been after, that it's overripe for that. But there's one danger in it. If Palgrave knows that's coming, he'll start to cover up fast. We've got to pull it off so fast he won't have the chance."

"Such as what something?" Pitt said puzzledly.

"I figure we ought to seize the courthouse and its records the first thing. Then ask the state to appoint temporary outside officials and step out, ourselves, till after the election."

"Seizing the courthouse," Pitt muttered, "sounds to me like pulling off a revolution."

"Maybe, but it's been done before." Nervous and restless, Lex ground out his cigarette. He thought a moment and was rolling another smoke by the time he had finished. "And I'd suggest another move at the same time — against Slick Ear Plateau to clean out what's left of it. There's where Palgrave figures to get what extra gun strength he needs."

"Palgrave thinks of everything," Pitt reflected. "He probably even knows what he'd do if we try to jump the courthouse. It won't be easy to pull off, Lex."

"It sure won't. But I can think of nothing whatsoever that would. Now, I'm going to see whether I can sleep."

"You go ahead. There's a man setting up at the bunkhouse, and I'll see if Amy will let me spell her with Holly. Which I doubt."

Lex grinned. "It took doing to get them next to each other. But now they've sure got it bad."

"They sure have. How do you feel about it, man?"

"It's fine."

"Thank God you feel that way. Now you hit your soogans."

Although he had figured himself too churned-up to sleep, Lex dropped off as soon as he had crawled into bed. When he opened his eyes it was again day, and he found his strength and drive restored. He rose to find that Pitt had already picked a crew for the job of returning the stolen cattle to their home range. Lex hurried through his own breakfast and saddled a horse to join them, eager for a turn at something normal and productive only of routine results. The little outfit moved out at once and had no difficulty in rounding up the steers found on the backland plateau.

The Toadstool riders carefully skirted the shot-up camp there and the dead men still lying about. Conbuck had promised to send a wagon for them, and now the Starlight punchers wanted to steer clear of any machine men whatsoever. By late afternoon the rustled cut had been thrown back on its own range. With the dead buried and the wounded cared for the ranch had recovered as far as possible from the effects of Hap Haber's raid. But actually, Lex knew, it had not and would not return to normal until the larger struggle was settled. Every man on the spread awaited a new dusk and the resumption of that effort.

Basiners began to drift into headquarters in the shank of the evening. They were not a mob but orderly, hand-picked men sent in by the score of ranches strung down the length of Starlight Basin. That covered a lot of territory, but Ralph Turngate had dispatched half a dozen of his riders to bring them in. The fighting force assembled in the big ranchyard, stern and aroused men, many of them veterans of the old range war that now seemed never to have stopped. Watching them come in, Lex felt a mixed pride and dread.

Standing on the porch steps, he at last called for attention. Having no wish to arouse tempers beyond their present dangerous state, he spoke in the most casual manner he could manage.

He said, "You boys are loaded for bear, and so am I. Pitt told me there was sentiment, last night, for including the Kinsey Flat nesters with the enemy. That would only be a waste of lead and lives and, to my mind, a tragic one. They've backed the Palgrave machine all through the years, I know, but only because of that old enmity."

"What made them saints all at once?" Henry Cobb, of Horseshoe, demanded.

"Now, you wait a minute," another man cut in. "Lex makes sense. Palgrave's the man behind it all. And you sure as hell don't kill a wolf by chopping off its tail. We got to get the head and heart. Palgrave, Conbuck and Frank Renwick make that up. Let's settle that in our minds right now, then listen to what Lex has to say."

"I ain't forgetting the years them sodbusters have been Palgrave's pets at our expense," Cobb returned. "I ain't got over the range they chopped up when they come into this country. So I don't see any cause for us to bend over backward with 'em. This is a chance to thin 'em out, while we've got excuse." His heated face showed the furies that had simmered in him all down the years. It was contagious, for other men began to nod and let their own sentiments show.

Lex had an all-gone feeling, realizing what an unstable element human emotion became when men acted in concert in any factional cause. These denizens of the open range were particularly susceptible because the stakes had been high, the obstacles somber throughout their lives.

He felt the responsibility to harness that force, to tap off its dangerous excess to be his own. Through his weekly newspaper he had set out to unite that very element behind a sensible and restrained cause. If he could not do it now, he was a disgrace to the editor's role he had accepted. All that was needed, he felt, was a concrete plan that would let them vent their feelings and yet serve a constructive purpose.

"I'm no general," he said, grinning lazily, "and I've got reason to wonder if I'm as bright as the rest of you. But I mentioned something to Pitt last night he seemed to think was a good idea. It was to seize the courthouse and records, then ask the state to take over till after the election. That means ballots and not bullets, boys. Big John's preached that all through the years. It took me a long while to agree with him, but I do now. Violence only breeds more violence. That's proved by the fact that we've always figured we could fight the old war better and win it, if we could do it over again."

"You're damned catootin'!" Cobb returned.

"When would we go after the courthouse?" a man cut in.

"Tonight," Lex said. "Before any word of our intentions could leak to Palgrave's side."

"It makes sense. Let's vote on it right now."

The suggestion was inspired, Lex realized, by the speaker's own wish for moderation. Many another seemed to harbor the same desire, for he found it unnecessary to make a formal request for a vote. A yell

198

of approval went up at the very suggestion. Even the headlong Cobb and his backers accepted the situation and joined in.

The detailed planning began at once, and with the decision made suggestions began to come from all sides. They were constructive, designed to remain within the limits of the law to the greatest extent possible. Lex's further suggestion that Slick Ear Plateau be immobilized, and prevented from lending help to the machine, was also adopted. There were plenty of men to do both jobs, and Pitt Berts was selected to lead the contingent bent on entering the backlands in force. Lex and Turngate were chosen to head the larger party moving on Flat Rock.

They waited at Toadstool until midnight, high in spirits again and ready to eat the meal the ranch cook prepared for them. Then Pitt picked his men, ten of them, and rode out. Minutes later a force twice that size rose to leather and started for the county seat.

It was a serene night, with no wind and with bright stars flung in brilliance across the sky. Lex and Turngate rode in advance of the others to watch forward reaches of the land, since there was always the danger that Palgrave was keeping close watch on the basin, just in case. But they saw nothing to indicate that any of the machine men were abroad in the vicinity, and in the small hours of the morning pulled down at a distance from the town.

"We might as well light the fuse right off," Lex told Turngate. "Even if Palgrave's smelled a rat by now, our chances won't get any better."

Turngate agreed. He took a third of the men and pressed on, assigned to the task of gaining entrance to the courthouse and holding it until the showdown was over and the basiners could consolidate their position. Lex split the rest of the outfit into three small squads, one to tackle Staff Palgrave's well-guarded place and try to capture the man, another to do the same with Frank Renwick. The last, including Lex himself, was to call on Abel Jerome.

Lex waited for half an hour after Turngate had left, then led his own detachment on. When they reached the gulch outside of town where once before he had hidden his horse, he halted. He made a division of the men, appointing leaders, and told them the order in which they would move onto their objectives. He waited behind the others with only two men, not liking what he faced at all.

He had not fully communicated his suspicions of Jerome and Sara to the basiners. He clung to the dim hope that somehow they could exonerate themselves or mitigate their guilt. But this plan was dangerous to so many men besides himself that neither Jerome nor Sara could be allowed to run loose until it had been carried out. Because it was altogether too possible that he had played the part of a fool, Lex had picked that unpleasant job for himself.

The streets of Flat Rock seemed serene and empty when he rode in quietly with his two saddlemates. He could see nothing at all of the other basin men, who were carrying out their parts with expert daring. Yet as he came to the main street intersection, he saw that a couple of saloons were still open, their fronts showing light. When he had crossed the river bridge, turning out toward the Jerome place, Lex halted his little command.

"You boys just cover me," he said. "I'm only guessing, but it looks like we can pull off a surprise. So we don't want to do anything we don't have to that might tip it off."

The two men agreed, and Lex rode on alone. As he neared it, he saw that Jerome's house was completely dark. He left his horse at the outer gate, moving openly and as casually as he could manage. His knees were weak when he went up the path to the porch, but he was not challenged. The only difference to his previous call was that now, when he put his knuckles to the door, he had his gun in the other hand.

It was Jerome who responded after a long moment. He had pulled his trousers over his underwear but was still barefoot. Lex's hopes rose a little when he saw that Jerome had not bothered to pick up a gun before he answered the summons.

"You!" Jerome breathed.

Lex stepped inside, forcing the man to draw back. He said, "We'll leave the door open. I've got men outside, if I need them. Get dressed. Call Sara and tell her to dress, too."

"What is this, anyhow?"

"Never mind that. Just do what I tell you."

"Now, wait!" Jerome gasped. "If you boys aim to jump Palgrave, let me warn you that he expects it and is ready. That's always been a big threat to him."

"He got the Slick Ear bunch here?" Lex asked in sharp concern.

"No, but he's got a couple of dozen nesters here, all armed to the teeth. He's deputized them to the last man. They're waiting in the Wagonwheel in case they're needed. After you got Doc Cornell away from them, Palgrave knew you were apt to come straight at him next. Don't do it. He's got Conbuck and all of Conbuck's deputies, too. If you basiners start shooting, he'll call it an armed uprising and slaughter the last one of you. I'm not stretching it, man. Round up your boys and get them out of town."

"Too late, even if I believed you," Lex snapped. "Get dressed and call Sara before I roll her out, myself."

"She isn't here."

"Where, then?"

"Down at the *Call* office, with young Jimmy Kemble."

"With Jimmy? What for?"

"They're getting out an extra," Jerome said. "They figured they had all night to do it. You're going to ruin that, too, if you blow the lid off tonight." Jerome broke off then. "There's no use arguing with you, I guess. We'll go down so you can ask Jimmy what he thinks about us Jeromes now. I'll get dressed."

Lex still dared not trust him, and he stood near the man until they were ready to go. But there was no least show of belligerence in Jerome. He was deeply alarmed, entirely co-operative, and what he had said sounded sincere.

202

Although Jerome walked willingly from the house, Lex still kept his gun on him. He led his horse, walking behind the veterinary. Presently the two basin riders came out of the shadows and fell in behind. The town was still quiet, wholly undisturbed. But the other parties had been instructed to gain their positions, then wait for a signal from Turngate, which had not yet come. If Jerome wasn't lying about Palgrave's strength, the lid was going to blow off of Flat Rock at any minute, with the basiners finding it a much more costly job than they had estimated.

CHAPTER
EIGHTEEN

The *Call* shop was lighted, but the windows had been blanketed, which was why Lex had not noticed any activity there on his way into town. When they reached the place, Jerome strode confidently to the door, calling softly. The two riders with Lex sat their horses guardedly in the street.

It reassured Lex somewhat when Jimmy came to open the door while knowing it was Jerome who had summoned him. Then the boy saw Lex and cried, "Gee whilikers, am I glad to see you! Me and Sara figured we knew how to get out a paper, but we've sure been having a time."

Lex stepped inside behind Jerome. Sara, no longer neat, was trying to operate the big old press which something had stalled. She stared at Lex in quick wonder and at the gun he still held on her father. Then, frowning, she went on with her search for the trouble with the old printing press. Jimmy had been folding smudgy, wrinkled papers, and there was a small pile of them on a table.

"It would save time," Jerome said, pointing, "if you'd just take a look at one of them."

Lex holstered his gun finally, knowing that Jimmy could not have dropped his bitter hostility toward these people if he had not found plenty of reason. Picking up a copy of the new paper, Lex examined it in the light of the lamp. Clumsily produced as the thing was, it was still readable. His eyes ran over the first page, widening, stunned. The jerry-built headline was almost enough to stop his breath:

MACHINE MAN TELLS ALL. PALGRAVE EXPOSED FULLY.

Lex read on with bewildered eyes. Spread over the whole front page in big print was a detailed statement by Abel Jerome. It laid bare the innermost workings of the machine over the years. More important, it detailed one by one the calculated and vicious steps taken by Palgrave in the current crisis, not only for the purpose of winning the election but for the benefit of starting gun trouble in which he could rid himself permanently of his critics and enemies.

There was more, but Jerome cut in, saying, "We aimed to get those into the hands of the nesters who're in town, and get them to take more out to Kinsey Flats. They're all riled, but not many of them are fools. They know I've been a part of the machine, hiding the guns Haber run in to give them, and some other things. They'll believe what I say, and I figured that coming out with all this would deal the nesters out of the fracas for good and guarantee that Palgrave loses the election."

"In addition to getting you killed, Jerome."

"A man plays out his string."

"Who are you, anyhow?"

"That doesn't matter. Just let me handle this my way, Lex. It's something that's meant a lot to me for a long while."

"Believe him, Lex," Sara said simply. "It's meant so very, very much." Then her face went stricken, and they all listened in hard intentness.

From the distance, and in the direction of the courthouse, came the crackle of gunshots. A clatter of hoofs told Lex that the two punchers in the street had swung off toward the outburst. Jerome grabbed up what papers were ready and ran in long strides toward the door. Far across town more gunfire erupted, which would be at Palgrave's and Renwick's places. Lex bolted for the door, himself. He could guess that Jerome was rushing the papers to the nesters hidden in town, hoping to keep them out of the fight. If the man failed, Flat Rock was in for a bloodletting that sickened the imagination.

Even as his boots hit the sidewalk, Lex swung toward the river, wanting to be in on the finish fight with Staff Palgrave. When he left the main street he knew that the outburst had not brought the nesters boiling forth to help Palgrave. Jerome's strange newspaper must have given them pause, but Lex could not bring himself to trust that hope fully. Human passion was in the saddle here as it had been at Toadstool that night.

As he neared the bridge, Lex grew certain that Palgrave's place was the setting of a brisk gunfight. He had sent four men there and another four to Renwick's place, on beyond. It seemed now to be all one battle. When he came onto the bridge, flame spurted at him from the bank on the far side.

Lex let himself go forward onto the planking in a flat, hard spill. Thinking that it was one of the basiners guarding against support from the town, he called, "It's Starlight!" That only brought another shot hammering toward him. Cold went through Lex. It was a machine man holding back help for the basiners, who apparently had walked into a gun-trap here just as Jerome had warned.

Biting his jaw, Lex worked himself on across the bridge in a slow, careful crawl. When he reached the end, he held his breath while he rose slowly to a crouch. Again he saw the flash of exploding powder, now over to his right. But the man had been too quick, and the shot was high. Yet his position was such that he could keep anybody from moving along the road skirting the river.

Lex did not pause to think it out. Bunched legs drove him forward because he had to expose himself fully to get a fair chance at the man. Another shot burst out, and Lex fired at the flash. Then he raced on past the position and down the river road. No further shooting dogged him from the bridge position, and Lex hoped he had left the way open for more help for the basiners, if it should come.

The scene ahead was a starlighted area streaked now with searching gunflame. The thunder of the separate explosions rolled back in a mass wave from the high rock cliff. The basin force had thrown itself around Palgrave's big house, using the cover of the many plantings. The defense was hitting back hard from within. Lex swung in toward the cliff, not daring to come up on the street side.

As he angled toward the house again, presently, the shadows bulging ahead of him spat a sudden streak of flame. He was thrown half around by a thudding impact against his left shoulder. He shot at the flame and was not answered. His hit shoulder turned into a cold and alien thing attached to his body. The arm went numb. He shook his head sharply, trying to drive the paralyzing shock from his mind.

Crouched tensely against a bush, he understood that Palgrave also had men outdoors, that the intensity of the fight rose from its onesidedness in favor of the machine. Breathing heavily, Lex had a sudden sight of movement on the multigabled roof of the house. Somebody fired a shot up there, the streak of it searching down into the yard at an angle to him. He swung up the barrel of his gun, pulled the trigger, and saw a shape slide down a gully and fall the three floors to the ground.

He heard a shot pound out behind him. Another figure shoved into full view on the roof, then fell back out of sight beyond the ridge-line. Lex bent and cut quickly to his right. Three or four guns over there were steadily throwing lead at the house. The same kind of fire-streaked shadow lay around the darkened Renwick house, he saw. The gun in his hand was hot, and he could smell the smoke dribbling up from it. He studied the side of Palgrave's place from his new position.

All its windows were knocked in. No one, at the moment, was shooting out through the openings. He moved in closer. Then, across the gap between, the flame of a shot sprang at him. He felt the bullet go through the bloused side of his shirt and pass on, and he shot back by reflex action. Then he cut in to the foundation plantings and pressed himself into concealment. For what seemed minutes the only shooting was from the guns in the front yard. That began to taper out, letting the more distant shooting at Renwick's boom louder in the night.

Lex slid on to the back of the house, determined to get into the place if he could. He had not been challenged by the time he reached the back door. He began to hope that the ring of gunmen Palgrave had thrown about himself had been broken. The door to the back porch wasn't locked.

He twisted the knob and let the panel swing inward. There was no contest from inside, nor again when he stepped on into the kitchen. He went through that first room, slowly creeping and with his gun held ready. His shoulder was beginning to thaw out and hurt. He waited, then, listening through long and breathless moments. Then slowly he began to understand that this particular part of the fight was over.

He went on through the house, searching warily from room to room and finding it completely deserted. He found dead men and wounded, but Staff Palgrave himself was not there. A bitter futility rose in Lex.

Other men had provided Palgrave with this luxury, other men had died to defend it for him. But Palgrave had taken himself into safety somewhere — fomenting violence and escaping from it cunningly without self-damage.

Lex made his way out through the back, calling openly to his men to identify himself. When he was answered he went forward to join them. All four of the basiners who had been here were still on their feet.

"It's salted down here and was a waste of time," he told them. "Palgrave was all set for us. It seems to be petering out over at Renwick's, too. When the boys get it mopped up, they won't find anything but small fry. The bigwigs are probably at the courthouse with a sheriff's force and a bunch of lunatic nesters to help protect 'em."

"Sounds like it's settled at the courthouse, too," a man said. "I don't hear any shooting over that way."

"You boys help finish up at Renwick's," Lex said. "There's a slim chance they've really got something treed. I'm going back across town."

Walking along the river road at an unsteady gait, he remembered the man he had tangled with there without pausing to determine the outcome. He moved warily, ready to fight for his right of passage again. But there was no threat to it. He crossed the bridge and lifted his gait to a swinging run. The town side of the river was almost quiet again, with a strangeness in the lull that disturbed him. He swung onto the main street and saw it filled with men. They were nesters, but they

210

apparently were keeping together and out of the dispute.

They watched him closely, warily and even with open hostility as he pressed through them. Then he heard a cry and saw Jimmy running toward him, brushing his own way roughly as he came along the thronged walk.

Jimmy bawled, "Lex!" Then with a cautious glance about he fell silent. Coming up to Lex, he went on in a whisper, "You and your men have got to kite it quick. Conbuck's top dog at the courthouse. I done some spying and was going across the river to warn you."

"Do you know if Palgrave's there?"

"The whole kit-and-caboodle is there. With Conbuck and his deputies fixing to come and take the rest of you. I heard them talking, Lex — I know. Turngate walked right into it. The ones who ain't shot up are locked up now. Palgrave's labeled it a revolution and has sent for the nesters to come to the courthouse. But they ain't going yet. Our extra took some of the bite outta them. You light your shuck, Lex. They'll be combing this town in a minute."

"You get home," Lex said. "These streets are certainly no place for you, tonight. Go on, boy — rattle your hocks!"

Jimmy left, and Lex noted that several men standing close had been trying to listen in on the conversation. One held a copy of the little extra.

Staring at him, Lex said, "You've read what Jerome had to say in that paper. You know he was on the inside of the machine. You saw him deliver those papers himself and that the story must have had his full approval. He's told you how Palgrave's tried to use you like he uses everybody to serve his own ends. Are you still in doubt?"

The nester's face was set. He shrugged. "There's so damned much gone on that I don't understand that I don't know what to believe."

Nobody tried to interfere when Lex swung around and started back toward the river. He realized then that it had grown wholly quiet on the far side. When he reached the bridge, he saw the basiners coming toward him, seven strong.

He sagged against the bridge rail, waiting for them, reflecting that the trouble had started on this spot only a few days ago when Haber had beat up Jimmy. The seven men he saw coming toward him were all the free and able left of the twenty who had started out so optimistically from Toadstool that night. With the bunch Pitt had taken to the Slick Ear country, they were the cream of the basin's fighting force. Now they had a choice between hightailing it in utter rout or of staying and almost surely dying or being locked up with Turngate's men.

They could not run, Lex told himself bitterly. If they conceded defeat, Palgrave was in the saddle forevermore. At least a score of armed nesters and many men of the town itself were standing by, letting the men get away with it once again. Fury churned in Lex. While Jerome had managed to keep them from pitching in on the machine's side, they were not going to stand against the machine, either.

When his men came up to him, he told them what had happened to Turngate's outfit and of the new danger to themselves, concluding, "I suggested this. So I'll leave it up to you boys whether we skip out or make it a last ditch fight."

"Where's the ditch?" a man growled. "I'd rather fight."

A figure walked out of the alleyway on the town side of the bridge, broke step in hesitation, then swung onto the approach. It was Abel Jerome, Lex saw.

"You men have got to move," Jerome said. "One way or the other. You've got little reason to trust me, but maybe it's a case of circumstances making strange bedfellows. Palgrave's riding high in the saddle, but I think there's a chance to turn the tables on him."

"You raised a neat question, Jerome," Lex returned. "Unless you want to cut the deck deeper right now, why should we trust you?"

"One reason is that you know I'm a dead man, once the machine lays hands on me. They're not trying yet. They've been too busy."

"Then what's your caper?"

Jerome's gaze was full and steady, not that of a traitor in spite of all the unexplained things Lex knew about him. He said, "I told you that Conbuck's deputized a lot of nesters. Figuring to use them for fools, like I told them at the Wagonwheel. But they're still deputized. They're law and, man for man, far better law than Conbuck could have been even if he'd wanted. I didn't get far talking to them but I seen a chance. Somebody's got to persuade the nesters to take over as constituted officials of the county."

"Just try," Lex said with a snort. "I talked to one nester. All he could do was bat his eyes and swallow. It wasn't enough for you to put it in black and white in the *Call*. You forgot to put in pictures."

"They don't know if they can really trust me enough to take serious action like that," Jerome said. "But I know two men on our side I think they would trust enough to do it. Either Doc Cornell or Big John Starlight."

"Doc's out at the ranch, and Big John's a sick man."

"But Big John could cut the caper," Jerome said gently. "He's one cowman the nesters always respected. He's the one man Staff Palgrave fears. I know. And John's got a right to a part of this showdown. I know that, too."

"But he can't even leave the house."

"Let's go see him," Jerome said. "Send your men home before Conbuck gets ready to come after them. Then you and me'll make medicine with your dad."

"You don't know what you're saying. Big John would walk downtown if he thought it would help. And it would kill him. Damn it, man, he's a lot to me and Holly."

"He's a little something to me, too, son."

Lex looked at his men then and said, "Get your horses and light out for the ranch. I may be seven kinds of a fool, but I'm going to take a chance on Jerome."

The night's fury had so relieved the tensions that it was easy to walk the town's back streets undisturbed.

214

Lex had a sense of unreality, of disbelief in what he was doing, stringing along with Abel Jerome in a daring and risky plan.

Jerome said no more, and they came to the Starlight house by the back way. Lex called out softly to identify himself, then stepped into the kitchen. Jerome followed quietly, and they crossed two dim rooms to the big archway of the sitting room. Two people faced them.

Jimmy had climbed to his feet, a wide grin on his face. But Big John only let out a gasp as he stared at the man behind Lex. Shock had climbed into his face.

He gasped, "George — George Galtry . . ."

Jerome grinned at him. "That's right, John. Long time no see. Howdy."

Lex felt a wave of shock roll over him. So this was the wildling uncle, the reason for that nagging sense of half-recognition. So — and he could not bring himself to accept it — Sara was his own blood cousin. Had she known? She must have, from the start.

Jerome went on into the room. His smile was light-mannered but the look in his eyes was far from light.

"George," said Big John, "I supposed that you were dead."

"Not yet, but maybe soon. Maybe you with me, John. It's our big chance now. Yours to die for the decency you always stood for. Me for the decency I had once and threw away. But would like to have again — you've got to believe that."

"Why did you come to Flat Rock?"

"Palgrave got hold of me and made me come. He made me work for him. But he couldn't keep me from working against him, too. Jimmy must have told you about the paper they put out tonight."

"So it was you," Big John breathed. "He brought me a copy of that paper. There's more criminal evidence against Palgrave in it than anybody else could have dug up in ten years. Why did you do it after all you and him done together in the old days?"

"A man grows up," Jerome said tiredly. "Slow getting to it, sometimes, but he grows up finally if he's a real man. I haven't used the Galtry name in twenty years — out of respect for your wife and my sister. But time's wasting, John, and we've got none to waste. Could you get downtown in a buggy?"

"But why?"

Jerome looked at Lex, then. "You tell him. I'm a veterinary, but I figure I can do a fair job of fixing that shoulder while you talk."

In the excitement of the swirling events, Lex had all but forgotten his sore, benumbed shoulder. Jerome found it to be a shallow puncture of the flesh pads and gave it a quick, temporary treatment. Meanwhile, Lex explained to Big John their hope of persuading the deputized nesters to take temporary jurisdiction of the county.

As he listened, Big John's eyes grew bright. He said, at the conclusion, "Remember, George? Back there in the old days, Staff Palgrave swore by the gun, by the laws of force and dog-eat-dog. I swore by the law and lost every round to him since then. But this is another chance — to whip him with that law. We won't let it pass, I think. Jimmy, fetch me the rest of my clothes."

"You know it's a long chance for you, John," Lex warned.

"Long chance, hell — it's a *big* chance. Jimmy, get a wiggle on!"

CHAPTER
NINETEEN

His big arms swung across the shoulders of Lex and Jerome, John Starlight descended the steps of his house, moved down the walk and let himself be helped into the light buggy Lex had hurriedly brought from the livery stable. His gun was on his hip, his hat cocked well to one side, and if he never got back to his house again he was leaving it a happy man. The others caught his spirit. Even Jimmy, with all his love for the old man, grinned as he walked around the buggy and got in on the other side.

The town was still quiet. It was almost as if Big John was going for a pleasure ride with Jimmy. In a sense it was that, a fulfilment that had pumped new life into him. The buggy moved quietly to the corner and turned toward the main street. Lex and Jerome came along the sidewalk, abreast of the vehicle.

As it rounded the main street corner, somebody yelled. "I'll be Goddamned, men! That's old John Starlight!"

The buggy went on, Big John pleasant and relaxed, Jimmy sober-faced now but unflinching. Lex and Jerome shouldered their way along the walk, keeping up. A crowd formed behind and came along. The town understood. Staff Palgrave was at the courthouse, and here came John Starlight.

Presently John laid a hand on Jimmy's arm, and the buggy halted. John pointed a finger at a nester on the sidewalk and boomed, "Friend, ain't you Louie Andrea — the brother of Tom Lerner's widow?"

It was Andrea, who looked up sharply. "That's right."

"You been deputized?"

"That's right, too."

"Come along to the courthouse, then. We've got work for the law."

Andrea looked uncertain but moved along as the buggy started again. The incident electrified the rest of the crowd. Lex heard a man say, "Damn my eyes, I'm a deputy, the same as Louie! If John Starlight wants my help, he'll get it, too." By the time the buggy stopped at the bottom of the courthouse steps, the street was choked for a block about.

Mildly, Big John said, "Now, Andrea, I'd count it a favor if you'd ask Staff Palgrave to come to the door. I'm too old and too tired to climb them steps."

The uncertainty seemed to have gone out of Andrea. He swung and went up the steps to disappear through the double doors at the top. Lex was on one side at the bottom of the steps, Jerome across from him. The buggy was directly below the doors, angled in so that Big John could watch them.

Tense, hushed moments passed before anyone appeared up there. Then Staff Palgrave emerged, crossed the narrow porch in swift, arrogant strides and halted at the edge. He had been told who it was who wanted to see him, had been forced by the circumstances to come. Pride had kept him from lining his back with Conbuck's deputies. There was only Palgrave up there, and there seemed to be only John Starlight below.

"Andrea," John said gently, "arrest that man."

"What are you doing out of bed, John?" Palgrave said tauntingly. "Go back there and die. You're an old man — you're finished."

"Not yet. Arrest him, Andrea, and wire the U. S. marshal to come. The name won't fit, and the looks won't fit either, any more. But there are the scars of two bullet holes on Palgrave's chest, side by side. They'll fit a dodger the marshal can dig up out of his old, old files."

"The old coot's gone crazy," Palgrave said, no longer smiling.

"Then open your shirt," John answered. "If you ain't got two bullet scars there a dollar would cover, then I'm crazy, all right. Scars I put there the time you tried to stick-up a stage I drove when I was getting my start."

Palgrave's face had stiffened, and for a long moment he stood there staring down.

Andrea said, "The scars don't matter, Palgrave. What's important is what you've done to this country over the years and especially during this last week. Your hireling sheriff deputized me. But I ain't anybody's tool. You're under arrest."

Big John had won and in the way he had always yearned to triumph. Palgrave's searching look at the crowd below must have told him that. Then he looked long at Big John, who had a soft smile on his mouth.

Watching, Lex felt a surge of admiration for his father.

"I say that stage stick-up's important," a man yelled from the crowd. "It's a clincher on what he's done since. How about it, John Starlight? You really plugged him?"

"And thought I'd killed him," John answered. "It was in another country, and his name wasn't Palgrave then. I didn't figure he was still alive until he showed up here. That was back at the time of the nester war, and he hired his gun to your side. Then he turned politician, but one way or another he was always relying on guns."

"What kept you shut up about it, John? Why didn't you rid us of him years ago?"

"I couldn't. There was somebody — and a memory — I had to protect. Besides, it come to be an obsession between me and Palgrave. He always claimed he was too big for the law to touch. I claimed I could use the law to beat him. Lock him up, Andrea. I'll swear out a warrant afterward."

Andrea turned, but Palgrave moved first. His eyes narrowed, and his hand dipped under his coat. Lex started for his own gun, knowing that Abel Jerome was doing likewise. But Palgrave's eyes were on Big John, filled with hatred.

"By the gun, John!" he yelled. "To the end!"

A gun roared as Palgrave completed his draw. Lex swung a quick look to see the smoking weapon in

John's hand. Beside him Jimmy had shut his eyes and blown out his cheeks. Then Staff Palgrave fell headlong down the steps.

Softly, John Starlight said, "No, Staff — by the law. You knew it or you wouldn't have gone for your gun. And I proved to you once before that I'll shoot in self-defense."

Lex saw that Jerome was cutting around the corner of the courthouse, and he followed on the run. In a moment he understood the man's purpose. The back door of the building burst open. Only two men emerged, both on the run.

"Stand in your tracks, Conbuck and Renwick!" Jerome yelled at them. "I've wanted this a long, long time, myself!"

Jerome's voice only sent the two men into action. Lex had his own gun in his hand. Before he could line up his sights, both men had fired at Jerome, the man who had done much to undo them. Out of the corner of his eye, Lex saw the veterinary fold over. He saw his two remaining enemies swing his way.

He picked Conbuck, all the hatred he had felt for the man boiling out as he squeezed off the shot. Conbuck's momentum carried him into a forward pitch, hard to the ground. Lex shoved aside even as Renwick shot at him. The editor had a double-action .45 and got in another shot even as Lex fired. All Lex knew after that was that the courthouse tipped over on him as he went down . . .

It was a long dream, a bad one, and sometimes it was fraught with pain. Lex tried to wake up a dozen times before he finally made it. When he did, it was like getting loose from something on the bottom of a river and bobbing to the top. He opened his eyes to find that he was in bed at the Starlight house, with daylight filling the room. For a while he guessed the whole business at the courthouse had really been a dream — or else he was still dreaming. Because now he was the one in bed, and Big John was the one sitting in a chair, fully dressed, looking fit as a fiddle.

Grinning, Big John said, "Man, I never thought I'd get this chance. I'm going to pick you up and tote you like a baby and see how you like it."

"What're you doing dressed? You cheating on Doc?"

"Nope. He got in from the ranch. Took care of you. And discharged me. On the promise, of course, that I quit acting like hell on wheels."

Lex tried to sit up, but a stab of pain kept him flat in the bed. His head was bound and so was his shoulder. Now that the distracting tension had passed, both places hurt like fire. He remembered that last stab of flame from Frank Renwick's gun.

"How'd it turn out?" he gasped.

"The election's half over, already. The machine's clear out of business, and all that's left is to elect new people into office."

"Jerome?"

"You mean George?" Big John shook his head. "Well, he's dead, too — but square with the world."

"You were so afraid me and Holly might turn out like him. Well, we could have done worse."

"I reckon — but you got to admit I didn't know until last night how George had really turned out. It was Palgrave who led him astray, when George was about Holly's age. They teamed a while. That's the hold Palgrave had on me — the ability to slur your mother and her memory if I'd tried to use my knowledge against him. Weak, mebbe, but I could never bring myself to do it."

"John — is Sara my cousin?"

John gave him a sharp look. "What difference does it make?"

"Well, I guess I'm in love with her."

"Then you'd better ask her how it stands."

"Is she here?"

"She's taken over for Amy."

"I'd rather not have to question her, John, if you can answer me."

"All right," John said. "She's told me. It was her mother who straightened George up — that and the responsibility of suddenly becoming the daddy of a five-year-old daughter."

"He married a widow?"

"Yes."

"Thank God."

"It's quite a yarn, itself. George married her mother when Sara was a pig-tail girl. He lost her, same as I did my wife, and he raised Sara to grown. She never knew him except as Abel Jerome, a veterinary. Then, somehow, Palgrave found out where George was living. He sent Haber to fetch him. George had to come or be exposed to Sara. Which he was in time, anyhow. I was sick, slated to die. Palgrave feared that, in the end, I'd expose his outlaw past anyhow. He figured to have George here handy to use against me, if necessary. That was to be his hole card."

"And Sara found out how things stood?" Lex asked.

John nodded. "Yes, but by that time George had made up his mind to fix Palgrave in the way he did. But until he was ready to act, he had to go mighty easy for Sara's sake, if not his own. A man can't get away with half-hearted measures in a set-up like Palgrave had. George had to string along with everything they asked of him. But meanwhile he collected and recorded evidence against them. Sara also had to do a lot of things she didn't want to. But in the end she showed the same courage George did. Getting out that extra newspaper might have cost her her life."

"She's wonderful, John, and I could never bring myself to believe otherwise."

"That's something you ought to tell her — not me." Grinning, Big John padded out of the room.

Presently Lex heard light, running steps on the stairs. He had never seen anything lovelier than the girl who burst into the room. She had on a gingham housedress again, and there was an enormous happiness in her eyes.

Humbly, he said, "I'll never be able to square myself with you, will I?"

"Oh, you have — a thousand times."

"I never could believe you and — Uncle George were in it heart and soul."

"We were, darling — but on your side. You don't know how I yearned to tell you about it. But the situation was so ticklish for us I didn't dare. But . . ." She looked away from him for an instant. "There was something I wanted you to tell me, too — and you never did."

"I love you, Sara. I did from the start without understanding it. All that's been between us is good — so good I want it to go on and on."

"Oh, thank heaven!"

Gently she seated herself on the edge of the bed, against his body. Gently she bent until their mouths had come together. This tenderness between them was good, too, a balance to the fires that would run again between them. His good arm closed about her shoulder.